Praise for Craving

'Cool, sparse, and delicious, Esther Gerritsen's *Craving* hits all the right notes. This is an author who is unafraid of both complex characters and complex emotion (Thank God!)'
ALICE SEBOLD, author of *The Lovely Bones*

'With its deceptively simple yet extraordinary language and its sophisticated humor, *Craving* is a small gem among recent Dutch literature'
HERMAN KOCH, author of *The Dinner*

'Gerritsen shows an almost surgical ability to slice to the bare nerves of difficult human relationships. Elegiac, beautiful and very strong, it's a novel you devour in one sitting, drawn into the vortex as the inevitable ending spins nearer'
Daily Mail

'Unprejudiced and fearless in her associations, Gerritsen investigates the shadows of the human mind, meticulously, and with an eye for the beauty in the detail. Gerritsen's clear and light prose belongs to a new wave of literature from writers striving to capture human discomfort without melodrama, and to my mind, of these writers, Gerritsen is the most inventive'
Trouw

'Esther Gerritsen's characters have their own, extremely unique way, of viewing the world'
Vogue (Netherlands)

'Funny, moving and memorable, *Craving* is a wryly observed novel about family, human frailties and how relationships fracture'
EDINBURGH INTERNATIONAL BOOK FESTIVAL

'*Craving* is a harrowing story about the impossibility of loving and truly making contact with others, written so drily and pointedly that you regularly laugh out loud as you read. Esther Gerritsen excels at writing fast, humorous dialogue'
DUTCH FOUNDATION FOR LITERATURE

'Interpersonal communication is an inexhaustible theme, which she has so far managed to develop with great dramatic and indeed great comic ingenuity'
NRC Handelsblad

'Not only in her choice of subjects but also in her feeling for style, Gerritsen is one of a kind. Her absurdist logic and subtle humoristic voice make every sentence in her novels and columns a "typical Gerritsen"'
JURY, FRANS KELLENDONK PRIZE

'Gerritsen writes with style, wit and a sharpness that is eye-wateringly good. Her characters, whilst unsympathetic and very flawed are quite compelling to get to know'
Random Things Through My Letterbox

'Witty, sharp-toothed and dysfunctional, *Craving* is a darkly comic portrayal of a mother-daughter relationship. A fascinating, darkly amusing novel; Gerritsen writes with a calm and open hand'
Volume Books

'Gerritsen succeeds in constantly surprising the reader, right down to the final scene'
Cobra

'A writing style that grabs you by the throat: clear, rhythmical, humorous and sometimes deeply affecting in its rendition of the characters' trains of thought. Gerritsen scatters sentences that smuggle in the poetry in a seemingly careless way. She writes sharp dialogues that are at once hilarious and painful; and in doing so she touches places many authors can't reach'
De Volkskrant

'*Craving* is a razor-sharp psychological duet, with the mother's deathbed as the apotheosis. Played out through minor incidents, Gerritsen performs a grand drama full of absurd and grotesque twists'
LIBRIS LITERATURE PRIZE

'Esther Gerritsen's writing is probing, yet she puts into perspective the radical quests of her characters. This writer has a great talent for continuing to ask and to search, and prefers doubting wholeheartedly to knowing for sure'
JURY REPORT, DIF/BGN PRIZE

'The psychological context is beautifully worked out and the story creeps under your skin. *Craving* is written in an oppressive, dark and brilliantly turbulent way; it's a novel that stays with you and keeps on reverberating. You'll long for more: more Gerritsen, more of her writing style and more of that mystique she creates. Hats off!'
TESSA HEITMEIJER

'*Craving* is exceptional. By far the best book I have read in years. Stifling and comical at the same time'
VPRO

'The finale is moving and beautiful. It ensures that, as a reader, you are glued to the edge of your chair. This is a story that touches the very depths of your soul'
Leesfanaten

ESTHER GERRITSEN (1972) is a novelist, columnist, and scriptwriter. She made her literary debut in 2000. She is one of the most established, widely read, and highly praised authors in the Netherlands. Gerritsen had the honor of writing the Dutch Book Week gift in 2016, which had a print-run of 700,000 copies. In 2014 she was awarded the Frans Kellendonk Prize for her oeuvre. *Craving* was shortlisted for the Vondel Prize, and has recently been made into a Dutch film under its original title, *Dorst*.

MICHELE HUTCHISON studied at UEA, Cambridge and Lyon universities and worked in publishing for a number of years. In 2004, she moved to Amsterdam. Among the many works she has translated are *La Superba* by Ilja Leonard Pfeijffer, *Fortunate Slaves* by Tom Lanoye, *Roxy* by Esther Gerritsen and *An American Princess* by Annejet van der Zijl. She also co-authored the successful parenting book, *The Happiest Kids in the World*.

craving

Published in the USA in 2018 by World Editions LLC, New York
Published in the UK in 2015 by World Editions LTD, London

World Editions
New York/London/Amsterdam

Copyright © Esther Gerritsen, 2012
English translation copyright © Michele Hutchison, 2015
Cover image © Claro Cortes IV
Author's portrait © Paulina Szafrańska

Printed by Sheridan, Chelsea, MI, USA

Library of Congress Cataloging in Publication Data is available.

ISBN 978-1-64286-002-3

First published as *Dorst* in the Netherlands in 2012 by De Geus BV.

This book was published with the support of
the Dutch Foundation for Literature

N ederlands
letterenfonds
dutch foundation
for literature

Twitter: @WorldEdBooks
Facebook: WorldEditionsInternationalPublishing
www.worldeditions.org

ESTHER
GERRITSEN

craving

Translated from the Dutch by
Michele Hutchison

WORLD EDITIONS
New York, London, Amsterdam

FOR THE FIRST time in her life, Elisabeth unexpectedly runs into her daughter. She comes out of the chemist's on the Overtoom, is about to cross over to the tram stop when she sees her daughter cycling along the other side of the street. Her daughter sees her too. Elisabeth stops walking. Her daughter stops pedalling, but doesn't yet brake. The entire expanse of the Overtoom separates them: two bike paths, two lanes of traffic, and a double tramline. Elisabeth realises at once that she has to tell her daughter that she is dying, and smiles like a person about to tell a joke.

She often finds making conversation with her daughter difficult, but now she really does have something to say to her. A split second later it occurs to her that you mustn't convey news like that with too much enthusiasm and perhaps not here, either. In the meantime, she crosses the Overtoom and thinks about her doctor, how he keeps asking her: 'Are you telling people?' and how nice it would be to be able to give the right answer at her next appointment. She crosses between two cars. Her daughter brakes and gets off her bike. Elisabeth clutches the plastic bag from the chemist's containing morphine plasters and cough mixture. The bag is proof of her illness, as though her words alone wouldn't be enough. The bag is also her excuse, because she hadn't really wanted to say it, here, so inappropriately on the street, but the bag has given her away. Hasn't it? Yes? And now, so abruptly, Elisabeth is crossing the Overtoom, slips behind a tram, because it isn't right, her child on one side of the street and she on the other. It isn't right to run into your daughter unexpectedly.

The daughter used to be there all the time, and later, when she wasn't, Elisabeth would be the one who had dropped her off. Later still there were visiting arrangements and in recent years not much at all. In any case, the birthdays remained. Things had always been clearcut and she'd got used to not thinking about the daughter when the daughter wasn't there. She existed at prearranged times. But now there she was on her bike, while they hadn't planned to meet and it was wrong and had to be resolved, transformed, assimilated, she still has a tramline to cross, just behind a taxi that toots its horn and causes her coat to whip up. Her daughter pulls her bike up onto the pavement. The final lane is empty.

Elisabeth notices at once that her daughter has gained even more weight and blurts out, 'Have you had your hair cut again?' because she's terrified her daughter can read that last thought about her weight. Elisabeth likes to talk about their hair. They have the same hairdresser.

'No,' her daughter says.
  'Different colour then?'
  'No.'
  'But you still go to the same hairdresser's?'
  'Yes.'
  'Me too,' Elisabeth says.
  Her daughter nods. It begins to drizzle.
  'Where are you going?' is too nosy, so this: 'I thought you lived on the other side of town.'
  'I have to move out soon, the landlord's given me notice.'

'Oh,' Elisabeth says, 'I didn't know.'

'How could you have known?'

'I... I don't know.'

'I only just found out myself.'

'No, then I couldn't have known.' The rain becomes heavier.

'We're getting wet,' Elisabeth says.

Her daughter immediately goes to get back on her bike and says, 'We'll call, OK?'

'My little monster,' Elisabeth says. Her father had always called her that. He still did. It sounded funny when he said it. Her daughter gapes at her. Then her lips move. Go away, she says, silently. Elisabeth isn't supposed to hear and she respects that; her stomach hurts, but she hasn't heard it. Her daughter's short hair lies flat and wet against her skull. Elisabeth thinks of towels, she wants to dry her daughter, but her daughter turns away from her, one foot already on the pedal.

So Elisabeth is forced to say, 'I've got some news.' Done it. Her daughter turns back to her.

'What is it?'

'Sorry,' she says, 'I'm going about this the wrong way, it's nothing nice.'

'What is it?'

'But I don't want you to take it badly.' She slowly lifts up the plastic bag from the chemist's. She holds the bag aloft using both hands, its logo clearly visible.

'You might be wondering: why isn't she at work?'

Her daughter ignores the bag.

'What?'

'I've just been to the chemist's.'

'And?'

'It's the doctor. He said it.' She lets the bag drop.

'What did the doctor say?'

'That I need to tell people.'

'What, Mum?'

'That I might die. But we don't know when, you know. It might be months.'

'Die?'

'Of cancer.'

'Cancer?'

'It's an umbrella term for a lot of different illnesses actually. It just sounds so horrible.'

'What have you got then?'

'Oh, it's all a bit technical.'

'Huh?'

'It started in my kidneys but...'

'How long?'

'Must have been years ago.'

'No. How long have you known?'

Elisabeth thinks of the hairdresser, the first person she told. She goes every other month and her new appointment is for next week, in which case it has to be more than...

'How long, Mum?'

'We'll get drenched if we keep on standing here like this.'

'How long?'

'I'm working it out.'

'Days? Weeks?'

'I'm counting.'

'Months?'

'Well, not months.'

'Christ.' Her daughter looks angry.

'I shouldn't have told you, should I?'

'But... are they treating you?'

'Not at the moment, no.'

'Are they going to treat you?'

'If they can think of something.'

'And can they?'

'Not at the moment.'

'... and so?'

'Sorry,' Elisabeth says, 'I shouldn't have told you like this. We're getting soaked.' The bag is now hidden behind her back.

'So you... might... but not definitely?'

'You're not likely to live a long time with something like this.'

'Not likely?'

'Probably not.'

'Christ.'

'We'll call each other. Let's call. Yes? We'll call?'

And then Elisabeth crosses back over the Overtoom as quickly as she can. She slips and falls on the first tramline, but scrambles up again. As fast as she wanted to get to her daughter, this is how fast, no, faster, she wants to get away from her. The trams ring their bells and Elisabeth remembers the way her daughter had painted her room.

'I just start to paint when I feel like it,' she had explained, 'I don't put on old clothes, I don't tape up anything, because if I think about all the preparation, I stop wanting to do it. I just start, and then it takes me just as long to clean up the mess and get all the paint spots off as the painting itself.'

This was exactly what Elisabeth had just done. She had just started, at the wrong time, at the wrong place, in the wrong clothes. She had done it all in one go and now she would have to clean up the mess and hope that the result was better than before she'd started the job.

She walks to the tram stop without looking back and thinks about her hairdresser; her conversations with him never go wrong. Words exchanged between her and the hairdresser tinkle like loose change: short, quick melodies.

'The trouble I've been having…'
    'Go on.'
    'The pain in my back, you know…'
    'Yes, you said.'
    'Turned out to be cancer.'
    'You're kidding.'
    'Riddled with it.'
    'Aw, honey.'
    'I saw it with my own eyes. On the scans.'
    'And now?'
    'Now they're seeing if they can stop it.'
    'And can they?'
    'They're seeing.'
    'They're seeing.'
    'Yes.'
    'You poor thing.'
    'Don't tell the girl. You know – that you knew first.'
    'She doesn't know yet?'
    'I don't see her that often.'
    'No, right.'
    'No more than you do.'
    'She needs another colouring appointment.'
    'She dyes it?'
    'Highlights.'

There aren't any inappropriate words at the hairdresser's. As he dries her hair, they speak loudly. She can shout out words above the racket that would need to be whispered in other places.

Then the hairdresser hollers, 'That woman upstairs isn't doing too well!'

Elisabeth asks, 'What's the matter with her?'

The hairdresser says, 'Stroke, I think.'

Elisabeth: 'Talking funny, is she?'

The hairdresser turns off the dryer and does an impression.

Sometimes a customer will be sitting there waiting, a man reading a newspaper. Of course the hairdresser knows he can hear everything, but the hairdresser doesn't give a damn. The hairdresser doesn't talk to customers who aren't in the chair. But Elisabeth is bothered by their silent witness. One of the ones who always seems to be there. One of the ones who pretends not to notice but whose very existence makes things inappropriate.

MY MOTHER IS dying, Coco thinks, wanting to say the words out loud. She knows to whom and she is also looking forward to being comforted by him. The feeling in her stomach resembles being in love, she can still remember it from last year, though it might be hunger too. Funny, the way she can just keep on cycling; she still knows the way to the deli on the Rozengracht. Getting into the right lane at the big crossing goes as smoothly as usual, she takes the tram rails diagonally. It's not that she'd expected her emotions to make cycling impossible, she is far from sentimental, but she does long for a fitting reaction. She would like to stop and reflect, and this feeling does really seem like hunger. It's not that far to the snack bar on the Kinkerstraat that has RAS super fries, crispy on the outside, soft in the middle.

As she approaches the snack bar, she sees that the blue lettering on the façade no longer spells 'De Vork' but 'Corner Inn'—there's a new owner, and now she realises that the feeling in her stomach is not love, it is not hunger but panic, because bloody hell, they must still have RAS super fries, mustn't they?

It isn't until after she's ordered, 'One RAS fries and two battered sausages, please,' until after she's paid (did he hear her properly?) and the sausages have been dipped into the batter, and the man has turned his back and used the concealed RAS fries machine, that now she sighs, turns around, and sits down at a table in the window in relief, a view of the key-cutting shop on the other side of the street. She slumps into the hard plastic bucket seat, is happy, thinks calmly: what was that other nice feeling again? And is shocked to discover it is the news of her mother's impending death.

She stares at the safes in the key shop window, searching for appropriate thoughts, and is fairly satisfied with: later I'll be able to think, 'this is where I was when I heard that my mother was going to die.'

The new owner brings the fries and the sausages on a brown plastic tray. She doesn't take the food from the tray. She should eat slowly, ideally in a calm state of mind, but she doesn't.

When she's finished everything, she sits there aimlessly, staring at the key-cutting shop. As much as she'd like to share the news, you should wait with something like that, she thinks. And she knows that it's only half past three. His last client leaves at four, he gets home about half past.

'Apart from my parents,' she'd said, 'I don't know anyone who still has a house phone.'

'Yes,' he said, not for the first time, 'you're too young for me.'

Telling him over the phone would be a shame, she'd miss his facial expression. She'll call and leave a message that he *has* to eat at hers tonight, that she's cycled right across town to fetch truffle pasta.

Hans flies into a rage. Coco looks at the red flush on his cheeks and is happy, as though she's hit the bull's eye on the shooting range and a bunch of roses has popped up.

'She told you like that?!' Hans says, 'on the Overtoom?! "I'm dying" on the Overtoom?!'

Coco nods, wild, like a child. 'Yes, like that, just as I was about to cycle off.'

Hans is no longer leaning on the counter, he is standing with his hands on his hips, his belly thrust out. 'And then she left? Crossed the tram rails and that was that?' His eyes are enormous.

'"We'll call," she said.'

'We'll call?!' He thrusts his belly out even further.

'Yes, that's what she said.' Coco carries on nodding and just stops herself from saying: bad, isn't it?

'And that was that?' Hans asks.

The water boils, Coco turns down the heat.

'Oh yeah,' she almost shouts, 'whether I'd had my hair cut, she asked that too!'

'What a horrible woman! She must be a ho-rri-ble woman.'

Coco grins from ear to ear. She basks in the indignation he is so good at.

She says, 'Oh well,' and again, 'oh well.' She carefully lowers the truffle pasta into the water with a wooden spoon and waits for more indignation, louder exclamations.

'You can put the plates on the table, we'll eat in three minutes.'

'Oh well?' Hans repeats.

'Oh well,' Coco says, 'perhaps she was caught off guard.'

'Oh well?' Hans says again.

'Oh well.'

'Are you going to be like *that*?'

'Huh?'

'No, no, no.' Hans takes a couple of steps backwards, as though he wants to view the situation from a greater distance. 'This is typical of you. Feeding me horror stories about your parents and then playing it cool. "Oh well." And then you keep coming up with new details and let me do the swearing and then you go and defend them. I'm not going to go along with this. I refuse to have an opinion about this. Yes, well tell me, Coco, what do *you* think?' Hans looks triumphant. He doesn't lay the table and the pasta will be ready in two minutes.

'The plates,' she says. Hans gets the plates.

'Well?'

'Perhaps she shouldn't have told me... like that?'

'I don't know, you tell me.'

Coco looks at the clock on the microwave and feels like her party has been spoiled.

Hans doesn't stay. Hans has to work.

'A client?'

'I have to work.'

'Reading.'

'You can read here.'

'Sweetheart,' he kisses her forehead, 'I'll give you a call before I go to sleep, all right?'

She nods slowly.

'Or you should say: "It's very important to me that you stay."'

Coco doesn't say anything. She doesn't know whether it's important or not. It seems like a trump card that she can only play once. She'll keep it.

She met him a year ago in the launderette. A middle-aged man who didn't know how a washing machine worked. She had just loaded her wash and was wondering whether to go back to bed or go somewhere for coffee. She suspected that she was still drunk from the night before and that the headache would come later. That was when he came in. She was still crouched down next to the machine. He was wearing one of those expensive, long, soft woollen coats. He just stood there in front of the machine next to hers. He had a book and a newspaper under one arm and a large leather weekend bag under the other. He sank to his knees, the soft coat touching the tiles. He opened the machine and put his coloureds and his whites in together. The back of his neck was freshly shaven, still a little red, just been to the barber's. He stared at the machine, she stared at him. She wondered whether he had a piano.

He sighed and she wanted to say: give me your washing, love, come here, let me do it. As though she knew she would never see him this hopeless again, that it had to happen now, otherwise the man would just disappear from her life with his soft coat, his shaven neck, and his piano.

She began to speak to him very quietly, so that nobody would hear that she was helping him.

'You need to take out all the really white things. They'll discolour.'

He looked at her but didn't do anything. She felt it was an invasion of privacy to touch his washing but did it anyway. She pulled two white towels and a T-shirt out of the machine.

'Anything else?'

He slowly shook his head, no.

'Go for the coloured wash option at forty degrees. Here. Forty is always good. Or is there any wool here?' He shook his head again. 'Do you have any detergent with you? Or do you want the stuff from here?'

'From here?'

'It's horrible.' She took a box of washing powder out of her bag. 'Use mine then. Two scoops. In the drawer there. Right-hand compartment, left is for prewash.'

He didn't take the packet, so she filled the compartment with washing powder. She put her own softener in as well. He carried on watching her while she worked.

Instead of thanking her, he said, 'You're good at that, helping me, you've got didactic skills, you should do something with that.'

The way he was trying to turn the tables moved her. It made him even more helpless—a man unable to accept help.

He stood up and went to sit on a bench against the wall. He left his book in his lap, and opened the newspaper. She didn't tell him that he could simply give the owner an extra euro and he would put everything in the dryer and fold it up afterwards so that you didn't need to sit here and wait. She sat down next to him and asked for a section of the paper.

'Which part do you want?'

She didn't want to say that it didn't matter, so she said, 'Business please.'

She remained silent and felt his body warmth, smelled a faint whiff of aftershave. She pretended to read the stock-market report and tilted her head slightly to be closer to him. She wanted to rest her head on his lap, on that woollen coat.

She would have liked to have said, 'If you want, I'll stay home tonight.' She would never have to go anywhere again. She thought about her friends and how she'd be happy to swap them all for a man with a piano.

Even though she dried and folded her own washing that afternoon, she gave the owner a euro afterwards, along with her phone number, so that he'd call her the next time the helpless man came to do his laundry. She had loved him instantly, conclusively. So here he is, she thought, like a mother looking at her newborn baby, so here he is. There was nothing more to be done.

That second time in the launderette, she deliberately hadn't taken much washing with her.

She nodded at her bag. 'If it wasn't so intimate,' she said, 'we could just put everything in one machine.' She smiled at him girlishly, giving him the opportunity to play the conquering hero. He took her bag from her firmly and put her washing into his machine. Later on he'd say it had been his idea.

The first time they arranged to do something together, he simply announced it to her, 'We're going out for dinner. I'm paying.' It sounded like a gift. She was amused that he was ordering her around like that, and because she found it amusing, she didn't mind being ordered around.

He picked her up, he was wearing a suit. In the restaurant she tried to see what kind of body was hidden under the jacket. She loved his body before she'd even seen it. He told her about his divorce, which hadn't officially come through yet. He didn't have a piano. He loved the fact that she spoke Russian. He asked her to translate all the names of the dishes into Russian. She was much younger than him, but luckily there was one thing she could do that he couldn't. Without the Russian, it would never have amounted to much.

The first time they fucked, that evening, in his bed, in the small apartment above his practice, she looked at him, 'with large, frightened eyes', as he would later recall. It was fast. It hurt and she thought: if I don't think of this as pain, it won't matter if it hurts.

He even asked her, 'Am I hurting you?'

'No,' she said.

'You look as though I am hurting you; that's not good.'
She would try not to look like that.

'Why are you studying Russian?' he asked her, and she told him how it had started: that she'd read an interview with someone who talked about a book by Vera Panova and called it 'a friendly book about nice people.' The words had made her feel extraordinarily calm, as though she'd only just noticed that she was restless. The calmness was so overwhelming that she could no longer think about anything except the calmness, and the calmness became an obsession and turned back into restlessness again. She'd searched feverishly for the book, but it didn't seem to be translated into Dutch. One thing had led to another and now she was a third-year Russian student. As it turned out, the book had been translated into Dutch. They'd given the wrong title in the interview.

He'd liked the story. Back then he didn't know that the story would just fizzle out, that after three years she was still studying Russian because of that single line: 'a friendly book about nice people.' There should have been other reasons by now. She was like an old man who, after forty years of marriage, says something like: I married her because she had such beautiful hair.

Hans took her to museums and art galleries. They drove for hours for tiny exhibitions. He took her to restaurants where she was the youngest customer. There they'd drink lots of different wines, one after another. It was a way of drinking she was unfamiliar with. Drinking had always been a straight road, downing a lot of the same thing like you were learning a new song. Carry on at a steady pace, until you got there, until you understood it and thought: actually this song's not that difficult, did I really need all that time, all those glasses? The business with all those different wines was a confusing slalom through her head.

He asked her things, constantly: What are you thinking about now? What's going on? What did you feel? What does that look like?

At first it overwhelmed her. Often she would open her mouth and not say a single thing, afraid to put her thoughts into words. Until every answer seemed acceptable to him. Not a single thought was considered strange. It was new, as though she was speaking Dutch for the first time.

He bought her complicated clothes: blouses with horizontal pleats. He said everything suited her. And she thought: I could be anybody, but this is who I've become. She studied less and less.

It was nice when he accompanied her to her father and stepmother's. They got along well, he took over, she could just sit back and watch. He had never met her mother. He didn't go to the birthday gatherings she attended.

'I don't like parties, you mustn't take it personally.' Not that she did.

By the time they'd been together for six months, she had grown too fat for the blouse with the horizontal pleats. He didn't mind, of course. He knew all her Russian songs by now too.

The evening she knows her mother is going to die, she is on her own and eats Caramac and Toffee Cups in bed. These are the sweets she eats when he's not looking because she'd rather conceal her childish taste. She knows he is going to leave her. He can no longer bear how satisfied she is. He never needed to pursue her. She was simply there one day and he could have her. For a while things went well, he had just got divorced, and for a time he liked things that were unambiguous. A year of that was enough.

But now there's a sick mother; things like that excite him. It'll keep him occupied for a while. She won't die that fast. Perhaps while that happens, they'll be able to salvage something. Coco doesn't know how, all she knows is that there's still time and that's the main thing.

In two days' time they're going out for dinner with her father and stepmother. Coco pictures herself telling them. She is already looking forward to it.

In her mind she hears Hans asking her, 'What *exactly* is it that you're looking forward to?' But this time she doesn't feel like answering.

ELISABETH HAS TO drop in at the framer's on her way to the hairdresser's. It's still early, only Martin is there. One day the shaking just got too bad. She was standing at the big worktable in the middle—her table—she put her brush down, waited and then picked it up again. It was all right for a while after that. Then one day she ended up standing there waiting for the shaking to stop. The first time she took a sick day it felt like a longer wait, that's all.

'Elisabeth!' Martin says. He smiles and comes towards her, but she holds out both hands, holds them aloft in front of him.

'As soon as I've got something for the shaking,' she says, 'I'll come back.' They both watch her fingers trembling.

'They're just like little fishes,' Elisabeth says.

Martin takes hold of her hands and says, 'Good to see you.'

'I'm not crazy, Martin, I know I'm not getting any better, but there's stuff that can suppress it.'

'That would be good,' Martin says, 'that would be fantastic.'

'You don't believe me.'

'We could really use your help,' Martin says, 'it's the fair next week.'

'You don't think they can suppress it?'

'Elisabeth, that would be fantastic—we need you.'

'Well, don't count on it.'

Martin smiles.

'Why are you smiling?'

'Do you want a coffee?'
'I can't stop, I'm on my way to the hairdresser's.'

'Do you want much off?' the hairdresser asks.
'Add a few layers,' Elisabeth says, 'I'm letting it grow.'
'You're letting it grow again?'
'Yes,' she says.
'That'll take a while.'
'In two years it will have grown out.'
'Yes,' the hairdresser says, 'in two years.' They look in the mirror. He tilts his head to the side.
'What did the doctor say?'
'That I should tell people.'
'And are you?'
'I find it difficult.'
'Yes?'
'Yes.'
'I'll start with a wash.'
'I've just washed it.'
'Why did you go and do that?'
'Yeah, silly.'
'I'll have to wet it.' He rolls the sink under her head.
'How's the shop?'
'Busy, you know. Art fair next weekend.'
'And are you managing?'
'Not at the moment, you know.'
'No, not at the moment.'
'I shake.'
'I noticed.'
'Otherwise I'd be able to.'
He turns on the showerhead, 'Is that too hot?'
'No.' She always says no.
'Are they still treating you?'
'Not at the moment.' The shower goes off. Water runs down her neck.

'Finished the treatment?'

'Just having a break.'

'Just having a break, right.' The shampoo bottle is almost empty.

'Just enough,' the hairdresser says. He stands behind her and massages her head. 'Do they give a time frame?'

'You mustn't say anything, all right?'

'No. OK.'

'Is it getting thinner?'

'Can't really say, no.'

'Could be weeks, could be months. That's it, really.'

'But not years?'

'No, not years.'

'Does Coco know now?'

'Yes.'

'What did she say?'

'She was upset all right.'

'Course.' He turns the shower on again and rinses the shampoo off.

'She's getting big, isn't she?'

'Twenty-three now.'

'I meant "heavy", "large", "fat."'

'Yes, well, she just keeps on growing.'

'Right.'

'Fat people shouldn't wear their hair so short.'

'I said that too, but she wants it short.'

'*That* short?'

'Maybe not that short.' The hairdresser gets a towel and dries her hair.

'Why do hairdressers always cut shorter than you want?'

'Otherwise I get the feeling I haven't really done anything.'

'Oh, right.'

'You can sit up now. Does Wilbert know already?'

'I don't know. Coco will tell him. He doesn't come here anymore, does he?'

'Not for a long time. Used to see him in the bar here sometimes, but that was years ago too.'

'Doesn't drink anymore, does he,' Elisabeth says.

''Cause of that woman of his, isn't it.'

'Yes.'

'Maybe better that way.'

'Hmm.' She shrugs.

THE DRINKS HAVE been ordered already. Coco's father and stepmother (who prefers to be called Miriam) are still holding the large menu cards. Hans has put his menu down, his fingers on two different dishes. He wants the prawn chow mein, but with sole and a different sauce.

It suddenly occurs to Coco that it would be odd to wait until the starters with her news. She has already waited until Wednesday, until they are here, until they have taken off their coats, until they have sat down, but now she's got this far, her perfect timing seems banal.

'I think I'll have the *ti pan* sole,' her father says.

'Mum's ill,' Coco says.

'Ill?' Miriam asks. 'Have you seen her?'

'Bumped into her on the Overtoom.'

'What's she got then?' her father asks.

'Seriously,' Coco says. 'I mean she's seriously ill.'

Her father and stepmother put down their menus.

'What is it, dear?' Miriam asks.

'Cancer.'

'What kind of cancer?' her father asks.

'Kidney, I think. Is that possible?'

Miriam says, 'Gosh, sweetie, and you're telling us this now? When did you hear?'

'Monday.'

'Why didn't you call us?'

'I'm telling you now, aren't I?'

'Is she going to die?' her father asks.

'I think so,' Coco says. Hans is sitting silently next to her like a new recruit, patiently waiting for his turn to speak.

'Did she say that?'

'Not in so many words, but they aren't treating her anymore.'

'And you've been carrying that around since Monday?' Miriam says. 'Why didn't you call?' The waitress approaches. Miriam puts up her hand, like a traffic officer stopping a car. The waitress immediately slows down.

'Could you just give us a moment,' Miriam whispers.

'Shall we give the Indonesian rice table a go?' Coco asks. 'Seems like a nice idea to have the rice table for once.'

'Of course, sweetie,' Miriam says.

'Fine,' her father says. Everyone is looking at Hans now.

'Actually, I was really looking forward to that sauce I had last time and then with the sole, seemed like such a good combination.'

'We don't have to...'

'Let's just have the rice table,' Miriam says.

'It's for two or for four people,' her father reads out.

'What nonsense,' Hans says, 'if you can make a rice table for two, you can make it for three as well.' He raises his hand.

'Miss? Miss?'

The waitress comes to their table.

'We'd like a rice table for three people... and...'

'Rice table is for two or for four people.'

'Then we'd like one and a half rice tables.'

'It's only possible for two or four people.'

Coco says, 'We'll take it for four, it'll get eaten.'

'No, this is nonsense,' Hans says. 'Chinese is always too much.'

'We'll take the portion for two,' Coco says.

Hans gives the waitress a stern look and asks, 'But

why can't you make a three-person rice table?'

The young waitress blushes and repeats, 'It's only possible for two or for four.'

'But you do understand that this is nonsense,' Hans says, 'you can just adjust the quantities, can't you? I'd understand completely if you didn't want to do a rice table for one, but three is different. You just make a two-person portion a bit bigger, don't you?'

The waitress says, 'I'll go and ask.'

'Is this really necessary?' Coco asks.

'She's talking nonsense,' Hans says, 'isn't she?'

'Yes,' says Miriam, who can't stop smiling, 'of course it should be possible for three people.'

An older waitress comes to their table.

'You'd like the rice table?'

'Yes,' says Hans, 'we'd like the rice table for three people.'

'I'll ask the chef what he can do.' The waitress goes to take the menus.

'And then,' Hans says, 'I'd like the chow mein number 35, but with the sole, and the oyster sauce from number 42. Is that possible?'

'Of course, chow mein 35 with sole and oyster sauce.'

After the waitress has walked away with the menus, Hans leans back, grinning.

'See, you only have to ask.'

Her father has been playing with the beer mats all this time, he's built a house with them. The young waitress approaches with the drinks and a basket of prawn crackers. Her father quickly spreads the beer mats out across the table. The waitress silently places the drinks on them.

'Lovely, thank you,' Miriam says, still smiling. The girl nods and walks away.

Then Coco leans back too, looks at the spotless pink tablecloth, and again there's that fresh sense of delight she's been feeling since Monday morning. This time it's not only the dinner to come but the conversation. It is as though her mother, the topic of conversation, is lying there barely touched in the middle of the clean pink tablecloth. Elisabeth de Wit—wonderful conversation material even without an approaching demise—will remain in this company's thoughts all evening. The glasses are filled, the knives sharpened. Coco smiles and gazes ahead contentedly, looking forward to a predictable discussion, but one which will remain endlessly entertaining. Whatever course the story takes—a story in which she herself has a role to play—she will be the youngest, she will be the child, she will be innocence. Yes, this is what satisfaction feels like.

Before the first basket of prawn crackers is empty, they wonder, as they always do when Elisabeth is the topic of conversation, whether it's autism or, at the very least, Asperger's? It's an old question, they've been there many times.

'But there's never been a diagnosis, has there?' Hans asks.

'It's never caused her any trouble,' her father says, 'and Coco only went there one day a week and that was all right, so, well...'

'There was never any discussion,' Miriam begins, 'about where Coco would live. Otherwise we would have had to mention it, of course.'

'You did talk to her?'

'I didn't. Wilbert did, of course.'

'It still seems odd to me,' Coco says, 'suddenly getting a five-year-old.'

'I always said to Wilbert: Coco is welcome. Your daughter comes first.'

'She always said that.'

'It's still a bit odd.'

'Perhaps Elisabeth felt it was better too,' Miriam says. 'I don't want to pass judgement. But it was quite a surprise that she agreed so readily. I still remember Wilbert going round to suggest that Coco should live with us. I was at the shop. I thought: this is going to be a nightmare. But no.'

'No,' Coco says, 'I meant odd to suddenly get a kid.'

'Oh, that. No. No, I didn't find it odd at all.'

'It's not something you can just shrug off, you know,' Hans says.

'I'd known her for a long time of course. Wilbert would bring her to the shop if things got to be too much for Elisabeth, and I'd look after her.'

'What would happen—when things got to be too much for Elisabeth?' Hans asks.

'Oh, a lot...'

'Handy,' Coco says, 'having Miriam babysit.'

'I was happy to.'

'Staying home alone all the time with a toddler is quite dreadful, they say.'

'She was working too,' her father says.

'Yes, part time.'

'Why do you always stick up for your mother?' Hans asks.

'I don't.'

'Her lack of empathy may be a medical condition,' Hans says, 'but she's an adult who is aware of that condition and should at least try to do something...'

'No!' Coco shouts too loudly. 'That's not right! Her trying is exactly what makes it so terrible! When she'd suddenly phone, oh Christ, that was terrible. Thought she should speak to me.'

Silence descends. Miriam and her father look at each other.

'What?' Coco asks.

'We thought it was a good idea for her to phone you from time to time,' Miriam says.

'Was that *your* idea?'

'Our idea.'

'Yes,' her father says, 'Miriam thought it was a good idea.'

'You thought it was a good idea?'

'Yes, of course.'

'We can't blame your mother for doing her best,' Miriam says.

The young waitress lights the plate warmers and Coco says to her father, 'You married her.'

'That was a long time ago.'

'Was she attractive?' Hans asks.

Miriam says, 'She's still an attractive woman.'

'She's...' her father says, 'also a very easy woman in a certain way.'

'What kind of a way?' Coco asks.

'She doesn't expect much.'

'Bah,' Miriam says, 'cancer.'

'Are you going to call her?' Coco asks.

'Me?' her father asks.

'Yes,' says Miriam, 'you have to say something.'

The food is served by the young woman and the older woman. It doesn't fit on the table.

'We'll bring over another little table,' the older waitress says.

'Chinese is always too much,' Hans says.

'I think it's quite serious,' Coco says. 'She was carrying a whole bag of medication.'

'You have to call her,' Miriam looks at her father. Her father is filling his plate. The sole ends up on the extra table.

'Enjoy your food,' only the older waitress says.

'She doesn't have anyone, of course,' Miriam says. She loads up Coco's plate before starting on her own.

'I could go and live with her,' Coco says, joking, 'then I'd be nice and close to the university.'

'Coco,' Hans says, 'you aren't responsible for her happiness.'

Coco is about to take a bite but lets the spoonful of rice and satay hover in mid-air. She doesn't like Hans's tone and she doesn't want to have to say that she was joking.

She says it again, all serious now, 'I could go and live with her. It's a big house.'

'Coco,' Miriam says, 'your mother is a grown woman.' She talks loudly.

'You don't owe her anything,' her father says, pointing his finger at her.

'Listen to them,' Hans says gently. Her father and stepmother lean forward, towards her. Hans lays a hand on her leg. Coco is surprised by her family's bigotry. Is this her doing? She does love badmouthing her mother, but there are limits. She doesn't think of her mother when she speaks, all she knows is that she doesn't want to be one of these people.

'She's my mother,' she says calmly, 'and she's dying.'

'She's your mother?!' her father cries, 'Miriam bloody brought you up more than she did!'

'Wilbert,' Miriam says, he gets a hand on his thigh too.

'No one asked Miriam to bring me up,' Coco says. 'It was her own idea.' There's silence. Only her father eats.

'Your mother,' he says with his mouth full, 'your mother...'

'Wilbert,' Miriam says.

'Your mother shut you up, in your bedroom. When you were two. Two.' He sticks two fingers in the air and looks at her. Coco can hardly hear what he is saying, all she sees is his angry glare.

'You say that like it was my fault.'

'Do you hear what I'm saying?'

'Wilbert,' Miriam says, 'this isn't appropriate.'

'You're lying,' Coco says.

'I'm not lying.'

'Where were you then? How do you know?'

'When I came home you were screaming in your bedroom.'

'So you weren't there, you've no idea what happened when you were out.'

'Bloody hell, Coco, she locked you up. Two years old. She just locked you up in your bedroom.'

'Didn't you know?' Hans is almost whispering. She crosses her legs so that his hand slides off her lap.

'What happened next?' Coco asks, 'when you found me screaming in my bedroom? What did you do?'

'I thought she was over-exhausted. I stayed home for a few days.'

'You stayed home for a few days.'

'I closed up the shop, yes.'

'A week?' Coco asks.

'A few days,' her father says.

'Four?'

'Something like that.'

'Three?'

'Or two.'

'Or just one day?'

'I don't remember.'

'Just one day?'

'You can't shut shop for a week, Coco, you can't.'

'If you stay home for a whole day,' Coco says, 'how much turnover do you sacrifice?'

'Well, what would it have been at the time? Business was going well then, a day closed, that would have mounted up, you know.'

'If business isn't going well, is a day of being closed all right?'

'Then you can't afford that, a day closed.'

'Can't afford a day closed.'

'No, actually, you can't.'

'I'm going to live with her.'

'Coco, please,' Hans says, loud now, 'you're acting like a teenager.'

'You're only saying that to bug us,' her father cries.

'Darling,' Miriam says in much too high a voice, 'have you talked to anyone about this?' She looks at Hans.

'She's talking rubbish,' Hans says.

'Bloody hell,' Coco says, she shunts her chair back.

'We're only worried,' Miriam says.

'Why do people who say they want to look after you shout at you?' Coco asks.

They have some good replies to this, which take a long time to explain. Coco doesn't know what is worse—people talking too loudly or people talking too long.

Coco stands in the sitting room next to the dresser, the bedroom door behind her. He is sitting in his leather armchair, a glass of whisky in his hand, looking at her. She's wearing just a tight white T-shirt now and a new pair of pink panties. The material is shiny at the front, transparent at the back. She turns away from him slightly, buttocks towards him and waits for him to make a sound, a sigh, a groan. Nothing. She turns back. He's not moving. It's like throwing a stone into the water without any ripples forming. Up until now it has been simple. Just be young and pretty and take something off and he'd follow, take over, and she'd utter small cries of astonishment. Now he is massive, he has become one with the chair he is sitting in and she is an uneasy pink pig. Pig's arse.

On the way home on the bike, she'd said she didn't want to talk about her mother for a while.

She had tried to sound sweet when she'd said, 'Just let it drop for a while, will you?'

She arches her back. Buttocks out. Her stomach has got too fat for this pose.

'Are you sure you don't want a drink?' he asks. He'd already asked earlier. 'Just the one?'

She has stopped. It happened gradually. She simply drank less every day, at the beginning imperceptibly, nothing to worry about, but at a certain point she got down to a single glass a day at the most, and then that began to bother her too and she dropped the last glass.

'It doesn't agree with me, alcohol,' Coco says, 'you know that.' He drinks too much. Every day he opens a new bottle of wine, but she's never seen him drunk. He doesn't change when he drinks. She turns away from him slightly again, so that he can see her buttocks through the transparent fabric.

'Are you going to bed?' he asks. She has been sleeping a lot over recent months. The days are getting ever shorter, sometimes the day ends at nine o'clock already. She manages to send herself to sleep earlier every evening, like a skilled monk who can speed up and slow down his heartbeat. She rotates some more.

'Go and sleep,' he says. She's cold, her nipples are hard. She turns towards him. He looks into his glass again.

'I was thirteen the first time I got drunk,' she says. 'At the school disco.' She hears how childish the words 'school disco' sound and sees that that is the only thing Hans has heard—he doesn't have a clue about the darkness behind it. 'I couldn't stop,' she says, 'I didn't want to stop... I could do anything. I could think.'

He smiles. 'Get to bed, will you?'

'Mr. Polderman, my French teacher, took me home because I was too drunk to cycle. In his car... it was nice in that car. I could touch everybody.'

'Touch?'

'Do you understand?'

'No.'

'I wasn't alone. I was... I was with Mr. Polderman as well. Do you understand?'

'I think so.'

'Have you ever been drunk?'

'I know exactly when to stop,' he says, and it sounds like something he is proud of.

'My knickers are transparent,' Coco says.

'I can see that,' Hans says.

'Only from behind.'

'Oh yeah?'

'Look.'

'Yes.'

'They pucker up strangely at the back,' Hans says.

'They're supposed to.' She bends over slightly and uses both hands to pull the fabric tight across her buttocks.

'Look, that seam in the middle which is so puckered, it's intentional. I'm not quite sure what the thinking was, though.'

'Funny.'

'Weren't even that cheap.'

ELISABETH STROKES THE table. The old wood is scratched, there are dark patches where grease has soaked in, but the surface is clean. Elisabeth's eyes are damp, she is moved by the table top that she has just cleaned thoroughly and which is now so smooth, almost soft, like skin. The surface feels like a whole even though so many layers are visible: the pale wood underneath, the varnish, the spots. She strokes all the different moments in time and thinks about the frames she has gilded: pale wood, red underlayer, gold leaf, patina. The sound of the telephone behind her blends in with the table top, as though it is an object too. She doesn't move, carries on stroking, strokes the sound, before she... awakes? Yes, she seems to be waking up, but then in a new dream, because as slowly and carefully as she strokes the table, now she stands up, walks without haste towards the dresser, takes the telephone from it, as though she is doing this for the first time in her life.

'De Wit,' she says slowly.

'It's Coco.'

Her girl sounds light. Young.

'My girl,' she says.

'Mum...'

'Yes?'

...

'I'm... coming to live with you.'

...

'I'm coming to live with you, Mum.'

Elisabeth smiles, as though she's heard a strange, new word: livewithyouMum. It's because her daughter's voice is different from normal. Usually she sounds raspy and a little too slow, now her voice is clearer, and faster.

'I don't want you to be alone—now that you're ill,' the clear voice says. Elisabeth hears what her daughter says, but what she hears better is a lovely sound that she doesn't want to drive away.

So now she says, just as sweetly and just as fast, 'But that's not at all necessary, thank you very much. It's really very kind of you, but not necessary. Is there anything else you were calling about?' In the silence that follows she is afraid that her daughter's clear voice has gone again.

'Coco?'

But then her daughter continues, just as sweetly and just as quick, 'Hans can drop me off tomorrow afternoon … I've got a big suitcase here. Be packed in a jiffy.'

'Tomorrow afternoon?' Elisabeth asks—tomorrow afternoon is soon, tomorrow afternoon is real—'Hang on.' There's silence. Coco is waiting. Elisabeth has to say something.

'Hans?'

'My boyfriend.'

'I know that.'

'Yes?'

'Handy having a boyfriend with a car.'

'Great,' her daughter says.

'No,' Elisabeth says.

'What?'

'It's not possible.'

'I want to.'

'Oh,' Elisabeth says.

'I really want to.'

'Oh,' Elisabeth says.

'All right?' Coco asks.

'But of course,' Elisabeth says, because that's a nice answer. Don't think about tomorrow.

The stomach ache starts even before they've hung up. It's the stomach ache she hasn't had for the past twenty-three years. During the first few weeks after Coco was born she had it several times a day. Back then she didn't know whether it was fear or heartburn. The doctor couldn't find anything obvious. Her body slowly grew accustomed to it.

She'd come around one.

'Or do you need to go out?' Coco had asked. No, she didn't need to go anywhere.

Elisabeth looks at the table, the phone still in her hand. The table had been so beautiful just now. The table that had revealed everything for a second. Now the wooden top is dirty again, worn. Everything gets broken.

'Here I am,' the daughter says. Yes, there she is. On her porch, a large woman with a case, exactly at the time she said she'd come. Elisabeth wants to say 'yes,' but she can't breathe and just nods.

'Heartburn,' she says.

'Here I am then,' Coco says again. She looks young. She smiles the same way she did as a child. Elisabeth catches a glimpse of Hans's matt-grey Mercedes driving off. A lovely colour, she's never seen it on a car before. You need to give them compliments, children.

'It's lovely,' Elisabeth says, 'that matt-grey.'

Her daughter turns around and watches the car disappear.

She steps aside to let her daughter in. She presses herself into the wall to make herself small for that large daughterly body. The body doesn't move.

'Christ,' Coco says, 'this makes no sense.'

Elisabeth sighs and smiles.

'Damn it,' Coco looks at her feet. Elisabeth is still pressed into the wall.

'What do you want?' she asks her daughter.

Coco looks up. 'I wish it was normal, me standing here.'

'But it isn't,' Elisabeth replies at once, but then she adds, 'Or is it?'

'Damn it, bloody case.'

'Come in first,' Elisabeth says. Coco heaves the heavy case over the doorstep.

'Come in for a sec,' Elisabeth says again. She's coming in for a sec, she thinks, Coco's just coming in for a sec. 'A sec' is a nice phrase. Coco rolls her case down the corridor to the stairs at the back. Elisabeth wants to help her daughter, she has to want to.

'Just pop it upstairs,' she says, 'just pop it in your old room and then...'

'And then we'll see,' Coco says.

'Yes, we'll see about it later.'

Elisabeth watches Coco pulling the case upstairs, step by step, grinding it against the wood, as though the house needs breaking. A lot of weight is going upstairs but Elisabeth watches it in the way you watch something falling, something out of your control. A glass that isn't broken but soon will be.

When Coco is no longer visible on the stairs, Elisabeth turns to the gold-framed oval mirror on the wall. She looks at her own face and hears Coco's footsteps on the landing, in her old bedroom, back on the landing, now the bathroom. In the hairdresser's mirror her face is longer than here at home.

Her daughter was once one of those waiting clients,

one of those witnesses who doesn't appear to be causing you any trouble yet still makes everything uncomfortable. The older her daughter got, the more obviously she appeared to be observing things, as though there was something special to see. The older her daughter got, the stranger Elisabeth got. Her daughter made her strange.

Now it is as though the client waiting in the hairdresser's has had enough of the small talk, of all the politeness so he makes a fuss of putting down his paper and says, 'So, back to what you were saying just now...'

She hears her daughter coming down the stairs, and with every step she takes Elisabeth grows more afraid of her daughter's words. Her shoulders tense, as though the words were already pressing down on them. No daughterly words please, no hairdresser's words. She can do it, her daughter can do it, she sounded brisk and light yesterday, didn't she? Just a matter of finding that tone, hitting the right key.

'Sandwich?' she tries.

'Yes,' Coco says.

Good. A sandwich is good. Abracadabra, Elisabeth thinks, think light words now, just a sec, a sandwich, abracadabra.

It's not easy, people taking turns to poke their knife into the butter tub and the same jam jar. The sound of knife against glass, knife in jam. She misses the sounds of the framing shop, the dull thud of the cutting machine, the puffing of the underpinner.

After she was no longer able to work, she had wanted to say goodbye properly, but to the sounds in the household, the smells from the kitchen. She had wanted to put a bed in the shop and say: now it's done, now I don't ever have to go home again, now it's over at last and I will stay with the wood and the paint and the glue, surrounded by paper and glass.

'Are you afraid?' her daughter asks.

Areyouafraid Areyouafraid Areyouafraid, Areyouafraid Areyouafraid Areyouafraid.

'Yes,' Elisabeth says, 'I'll have a little think about that.' She knows if she answers too quickly her daughter won't believe her. Areyouafraid. Areyou Areyou Areyou. Of death of course. Ofdeath. Ofdeath. Or has she misunderstood again? Happens a lot. Just ask. A sec. Abracadabra.

'Afraid of what?'

'... of dying.'

'Yes—so I *was* right!'

'What did you think then?'

'I thought: maybe I was thinking the wrong thing, so I'd better ask. Does that make sense?'

'Yes, but what were you thinking about when you said you'd have a little think?'

'I was just having a think.'

'And what would it sound like if you did that out loud?'

Elisabeth opens her mouth, but doesn't say: Areyouafraid Areyouafraid Areyouafraid Areyouafraid Areyouafraid Areyouafraid.

Over the past year, her daughter's questions have got worse, ever since she got that boyfriend. Elisabeth might not see her daughter very much, but she always calls if there's something about Russia on television. She underlines it in the TV magazine.

'It's difficult for me,' Elisabeth says.

'I understand that.' Her daughter's eyes are shining now and she smiles cautiously. Elisabeth said the right thing.

She says it again. 'It's difficult for me.' Her daughter nods. Elisabeth nods too.

She repeats, 'difficult,' and pulls a troubled face.

'I told Dad.'

'Oh?' Elisabeth says. 'When did you tell him?'

'Wednesday.'

Three days. Wilbert has already known for three days that she's dying and she hasn't heard from him. He loves her, if he didn't love her he would have called her, that's what people do, that's polite. He isn't polite, he loves her.

'The poor man,' she says and then in response to Coco's confused expression, she adds, 'Is he still working so hard?' He had the shop before Coco was born. He always talked about it in a worried way. If it was too busy, he definitely had to be there. If everything was just running normally, it was better that he was there. When Coco was in hospital, after her fall from the window, he found it difficult to find time to visit her. Elisabeth had adopted his worried tone.

'Where is your husband?' the doctor had asked.

'Own shop, you know,' Elisabeth had said, as though it was a very serious matter.

'What kind of a shop?' the doctor had asked.

'What we sell,' Elisabeth, who never sold anything, had begun, 'are all the things you need for the kitchen but that you don't see on the table. So we have big knifes, but not normal cutlery. We have pans but no dishes. Chopping boards but not plates.'

'A kitchen shop?' the doctor asked.

'No, a cookery shop.'

COCO HAD ASKED Hans whether he would take her to her mother's. Her case was too big for the bike or a tram. They were sitting in a restaurant when she brought it up. They were eating 'tomatoes cooked five ways'. He said he wouldn't drop her off because he didn't agree with her decision. 'A misguided urge to rescue someone' is what he had called it earlier. He didn't think it would be good for her, he refused to help.

'Do you understand?'

She nodded. It sounded reasonable.

'I wouldn't give a robber a lift to the bank, would I?'

She felt insulted that he was fobbing her off with such a bad example. She decided to win this argument. Not because she thought she was right but because she wanted to win it, and because she didn't feel like getting on the tram with her luggage.

She tried to stay calm, opening with, 'This tomato mousse is delicious,' and only then, 'You're arrogant.'

'What makes you say that?'

'You can't only help your friends when they do things your way, can you? It's not like you'd say: I won't help you to move house because I don't like the look of the house you're moving into, or the man you're moving in with isn't to my taste.'

'You would say that if the man was violent.'

'My mother isn't violent and I'm not about to rob a bank, we're not talking about extreme circumstances or psychiatric cases and I'm not one of your clients.'

He ate with his mouth open and she knew she'd say something about it if she didn't win the argument. He changed his mind faster than she'd expected.

Even before the second course had arrived, he said, 'You're right. I'll drop you off. It is arrogant. Thank you for pointing that out to me.'

He looked so very smug, she said, 'You shouldn't eat with your mouth open.' She regretted it at once. His injured look was unbearable. It was like he could make his eyes glisten at will. The way the eyes of pregnant women or wounded animals glistened, the ones needing the flock's protection (her optician had told her that once when she needed new lenses). Hans did nothing to conceal his vulnerability and she hated him for it. For god's sake, you should be able to tell your boyfriend not to eat with his mouth open. Why couldn't he just take it on the chin? Why was he eating with his mouth open in a Michelin restaurant? And she hated herself for being so blunt.

'Sorry,' she said again and only later asked him whether he could do tomorrow afternoon. He could, but he didn't have much time.

'I'll drive you over but I'll have to drop you and run.'

Coco is lying on her bed, in her old bedroom, she calls Hans. She asks whether he'd like to come and have lunch with her and her mother.

'Let's eat somewhere else,' Hans says.

'Will you pick me up?' she asks. 'Then you can meet my mother.'

Silence. He doesn't want to meet her mother.

'Why don't you want to meet her?'

'Oh, I don't mind meeting her... if it's important to you.'

'Why don't you want to meet her?'

'You're reading too much into it. She simply doesn't interest me.'

She's heard him say this before about people. It's the worst thing he can say about anyone, Coco thinks. She suspects that it's his greatest fear, that someone might say that about him, but Coco knows Hans will dismiss this as Freudian nonsense. She feels stupid when he calls her insights 'Freudian nonsense,' so she often holds her tongue and pretends she's in a relationship with an extremely balanced man. Sometimes she really believes it.

'You don't want to meet her.'

'I don't need to.'

'What are you afraid of?'

'I'm sorry, sweetheart, but I'm not interested in your mother.'

She doesn't believe him. What she does believe is that she won the previous argument and that he'll win this one. She's not sure which of them is right, but she does know that it's a competition and that they are adversaries.

They are sitting in the Holland Bakery on the corner of her mother's street, at the long table in front of the window, side by side. Coco has ordered a cervelat sandwich because she wants to know what cervelat is. Hans wants a croquette sandwich without butter. Coco presses her fingers to her temples.

'What's the matter?' Hans asks.

'What do you mean?'

'Are you tired?'

'Why?'

'What's up?'

Coco is quiet for a minute. The waitress brings coffee. 'Headache,' Coco says.

'You couldn't say that right away?'

'It's not that bad.'

'Have you drunk anything yet?'

'Huh?'

'You always forget to drink.'

'Oh well.'

'Have you drunk anything yet today? Do you know how much a person should drink?' Hans gets up and goes to the counter to ask for a glass of water. He passes her the glass.

Coco is annoyed but feels thirsty when she sees the water. She takes it and drinks it.

'You were thirsty.'

'Yes.'

'Don't you notice then? When you're thirsty? How does that work?'

'Don't seem to,' Coco says.

'That's odd.'

'Sorry.'

'Why are you apologising?'

'Shut up,' Coco says, 'shut up.' She stares mutely into the distance. A truck stops outside. Large crates of meat are unloaded. 'Shall we go to a matinee?' she suggests.

'Do you think you'll be able to study at your mother's?'

'Want to come?'

'I've got a client this afternoon.'

'Cancel them.'

'I can't. And I wouldn't want to.'

'You didn't have to say that last bit.'

'I don't want to cancel my client.'

The waitress arrives with the sandwiches.

'I know you don't want to,' Coco says, 'and I'm pretty sure I know why.' She says it as though there's something shameful about it. 'It's because your job gives you so much satisfaction.' The tone of her voice alarms her. The disdain, the disgust. She quickly takes a bite of her sandwich. 'It's a kind of salami,' she says about the cerve-lat, 'but then without the herbs, without the garlic, and it's softer.'

'How bad is your mother's health now?'

'You don't have to stay with me just because my mother's ill.'

'How can you say a thing like that?'

'You can think it, can't you?'

'Yes, you can.'

'It's nice,' Coco says, 'that we can be so totally open.' Then Coco sees her mother.

She's walking very slowly along the opposite side of the street towards the paper-recycling container with a small plastic bag. Coco notices how thin she is. A small pile of paper emerges from the bag, she throws it into the container, and after that she folds up the plastic bag. The precision and seriousness of the operation is painful to Coco. These are the important events in her mother's life now. This isn't just what happens in between, it counts.

'You know, it wouldn't matter,' Hans begins, his voice is gentle, caring, 'if you changed your mind. I get that you want to give it a try, but don't be embarrassed to change your mind.' He strokes her cheek with the back of his hand. She looks at him and then at her mother. Her mother crosses the street again, agonizingly slowly. Now she should say it. That's my mother.

'You're such an arrogant bastard,' she says, laughing.

'You shouldn't say things like that,' he says, 'not even as a joke.'

His reasonableness makes her furious. His damp eyes make her equally furious. A hidden, sensitive soul that mustn't be offended. Cloaked in that eternal arrogance, the perfect double-edged sword for keeping her captive.

She watches him cycle away, one leg of his new jeans in his sock. He cycles off without looking back. A middle-aged man on a racing bike with a job that gives him satisfaction. It's easy to think scornful things about him when the eyes aren't there.

'You and your fucking clients,' she whispers. She eats the last mouthfuls of her cervelat sandwich.

She doesn't know whether the cervelat tasted nice. It tasted of water, the bread did too. And the milk.

She orders freshly-squeezed orange juice. The juice tastes of water too.

She orders a sandwich with warm beef and satay sauce. Everything is water. She tastes it and she understands it. Of course. We have to invent the flavours ourselves, we have to do it ourselves.

'COCO,' ELISABETH SAYS in the morning as she sits down on her daughter's bed, 'I think I'm getting ill.'

Coco doesn't respond.

She says it again, 'I think I'm getting ill.'

Coco sits up and looks at her now, her eyes popping, as though she's just been given some important piece of information.

'Didn't you understand me?'

'You think you're *getting* ill?'

When she woke up, Elisabeth realised at once that she wasn't alone in the house. It was like when she used to feel her husband's body next to hers, someone she only had to roll over and face, someone she could start to speak to, or continue to speak to, as if following a brief hiatus. The night seemed a mere detail, a brief moment. She liked people she could talk to. The people didn't necessarily have to listen to her, that wasn't the point, but they should be there. She didn't talk to herself, she wasn't weird. In the final years of their marriage, Wilbert began to complain that she told him things more than once: twice, three times, four times even.

'But I've known you for ten years now,' she once said, 'I can't keep on inventing new things, can I?'

'You talk to me, but it's like you could be talking to anybody.'

'I like to talk to you.'

'But you're not interested in my reaction.'

'But I'm not interested in anyone else's reaction either.'

'It's not right.' He said that quite often.

Something wasn't right. They weren't right together. She wasn't right. She learned to hold her tongue, to think before she said anything to him.

But when she'd woken up this morning, after her sleep had been repeatedly disturbed by an extremely unpleasant feeling in her throat and she'd realised at once that she wasn't alone in the house, she'd felt her old enthusiasm returning. Having someone to talk to was a wonderful thing.

She had got up at once, her eyes barely open, shuffled across the landing, knocked on the door of the children's bedroom. She hadn't waited for an answer, opened the door, asked, 'Coco, are you awake yet?' and sat down on the bed.

It was strange, how standing had become difficult one day. It's like the time comes when you're no longer a child and you no longer run, and the time comes when you're a grown-up and you prefer not to stand. At her work, she'd pulled up a stool and then it had become difficult. The frames were too big to do the work sitting down.

The large daughterly body in the bed rolled over, the eyes opened, and Coco immediately covered them with her hand. Elisabeth shrank back as though she was a lamp shining too brightly in her daughter's eyes.

'You think you're getting ill?' Coco asked again.

'Yes, I think I'm getting ill. I've got that thing you get when you're getting sick. It always happens in the same order. First indigestion and then a sore throat, and then coughing, after that I get a cold, and then I get hoarse. Or the other way round. But it's always the complete works. And still you think—maybe it will only be this bit, but it never is. I've got indigestion and a sore throat. Do you know if it's going around?'

Coco slowly shakes her head, so minimally that it's almost undetectable, that you can't accuse her of doing it, and still it makes everything uncomfortable.

'Why are you acting so strangely?' Elisabeth asks. Because why couldn't the child be the reason? Why can the child never be the guilty party? All those years when life was normal, the child's been here for less than a day and everything has gone weird again.

'You think you're getting ill?' her daughter repeats.

'I know I am,' Elisabeth says.

'Shall I call the GP?'

'What do you mean?'

'So that I know what's going on. What I should do.'

'Oh, they can't do anything, you know, if there's anything new they'll let me know.'

'The GP will?'

'The oncologist.'

'But now you think... that you're ill... getting sicker.'

'I'm only talking about having a cold, don't make a mountain out of a molehill.'

Coco closes her eyes.

'It was either the bronze paint or the thinner. I didn't like to wear those masks. That would have had an effect in the end, wouldn't it?'

Coco doesn't open her eyes.

'Are you tired?'

'Not really,' Coco says.

'You look it though.'

'Thank you.'

'Oh, sorry.'

'I was asleep.'

'Oh, you were still asleep, I didn't realise.' Elisabeth struggles to her feet. 'I just wanted to know whether it was going round.' She walks to the door.

'It's always going round, Mum, I've never been sick and then someone went, "How can you be? It's not going around." It's always going round.'

'And yet it isn't,' Elisabeth says, leaving the bedroom.

Later that evening, there is a wet towel over the back of one of the wooden kitchen chairs. Elisabeth looks at her daughter on the other side of the table.

Coco says, 'So you don't work anymore?'

'I wouldn't have a problem working if my hands didn't shake so much.'

'Do they?'

'Look.' Elisabeth holds out her hands, looks at her shaking fingers for an instant, turns her head and looks at the wet towel hanging over the chair. The chairs are old, the varnish is no longer as tough as it used to be. Damp is disastrous. She thinks this as though it's part of an advertising campaign. *Damp Is Disastrous.*

Sometimes a customer drinks coffee in the workshop and then walks close to her desk with his coffee mug. It feels like someone threatening to lay a hand on your buttocks and you have to hold steady, you have to protect your body. But her desk at work is large, she can't screen it off, guard it, wrap her arms around it. Sometimes it's a shame that there are customers.

'Are you getting disability benefits then, or how does it work?'

'Martin's sorting that all out, he's fixing it.' Martin, her boss, has increasingly taken over more of her work, her responsibilities – because they weren't getting done and someone had to do them. It had begun during the divorce. Back then they'd already started keeping her away from the paperwork at work.

'Let her do her work,' Martin had said, 'and nothing

else.' She worked more quickly than anyone else, but she couldn't fill out a form. If she started on something it was enough for her to remember that she needed the pink piece of paper, the job ticket.

'You mustn't do anything without a ticket,' Martin always called out.

Elisabeth would take a pink form and give it to a colleague who would fill everything in.

Sometimes Elisabeth would take paperwork home with her. Tax forms, insurance stuff. During the divorce the paperwork increased. In the end, Martin did everything.

Elisabeth looks at the wet towel on the wooden chair. A familiar feeling of resignation comes over her. The thing she'd once called motherhood. Being a mother was looking on as the child tarnished everything in the house, bit by bit, and letting it happen. Early on in life Coco seemed to take pleasure in moving things that didn't want to be moved. Bread amongst the puzzles, cheese spread on books, beads in the seams of the couch. Coco licked windowpanes, cupboard doors, and chair legs, rubbed slices of gingerbread cake along the walls as though using a sponge. Elisabeth was the road-sweeper's truck. Tidying up, rescuing what still could be rescued. She didn't know how to steer the child, what she did know was how to put everything back in place as fast as possible.

When Wilbert came home, she wanted the house to be clean and for herself to be clean and for herself to be his girl and for him to be able to get a bottle of beer from the fridge blindfolded, because they were always in the same place, restocked with punctuality, always cold.

He would drink his beer as she stood by the counter and, she might, she still remembers, use a finger to stir a green earthenware pot in which raisins were soaking in hot water. It wasn't necessary, what she was doing with her finger, but she had to stand there, with her buttocks jutting just a little too far out, so that he'd be compelled to touch them, to grasp them.

Then he would come and stand behind her and say: 'Oh Jesus,' always just 'Oh Jesus,' as though he were a victim of the buttocks. She wore a skirt that he could easily lift up. He would grip her hips firmly with both hands and tilt them, in an almost technical way, just as he would skilfully open a beer bottle with a lighter, or demonstrate kitchen equipment in the shop. A handyman, she thought then, not really a salesman. He should do something with his hands. She rested her forehead against the kitchen cupboard, both hands on the counter. She felt his cock against her buttocks. He pushed her panties aside, and she peeked back over her shoulder and saw how he bent his knees slightly, how strong his legs were, how he got everything at exactly the right angle. She observed it all with intense concentration. She paid attention. She paid close attention and she heard the child in the sitting room, allowed to watch episodes of the *Daily Fable* at this time of day. She had recorded a whole series of them. *Hello there, Mr. Owl, what's happening today in Fable Land? More news from our Fable Land.* And then his cock, which was strong and tireless, found its way into her. She tipped her hips a little more and smiled, so friendly and loving. She felt good, like a lovable person, a nice woman, a good mother, and there was nothing wrong with her. Everything fit.

He fucked her and said, 'Oh Jesus, oh Jesus, that ass. Oh Jesus,' and she thought: *aaba* and then she knew he'd been drinking, because he only spoke in *aaba* rhyme schemes when he was drunk. As well as feeling lovable and good and normal, she also felt strong if she kept her balance as he thrust harder into her. And when he ejaculated in her it felt warm, and only then did she think about what the child had soiled that day, about jam and milk and chocolate spread, about spit and snot.

His head rested on her shoulder and he said, 'What are you doing with me? What are you doing with me? I'm no good. What are you doing with me?'

She said, 'You, you, you are my love, you.'

And he answered in the perfect form: 'I'm no good for you, I'm no good for you, Elisabeth, I'm no good for you.'

And if he was very drunk, she said, 'You, you, you are my dog, you.'

She fed husband and child, took the child to bed, spent a long time afterwards clearing up the traces, and poured him drinks. The bottle of jenever in the cupboard above the fridge was never empty either. He would sit there and watch snooker or football. She refilled his glass. It was impossible not to want to quench his thirst. They were equally tired when they went to bed at ten o'clock.

But one day, Elisabeth was already tired at three o'clock in the afternoon. She watched Coco once again spreading pools of orange squash with the palms of her hands over the same kitchen table they were sitting at now, with a high-pitched moan as though this was causing her to suffer too and she hoped that someone would rescue her from this activity. It was then that Elisabeth realised it wasn't giving her daughter any pleasure. Her daughter was not creating something but destroying it. She soiled, broke, and tore.

If this behaviour brought her daughter so little pleasure and she herself had so much to gain if the child stopped it, it was reasonable to insist that her daughter change her behaviour. Or, at the very least, she could limit it to one room.

Long before the child was two years old, Elisabeth would shut it up, just in the bedroom. It didn't cry any louder, nor longer, than when it was with its mother. Elisabeth had checked.

She stopped shutting her daughter up when she was two and a half. Elisabeth knew that people can remember experiences from that age onwards. Although her daughter wasn't unhappier in her room than with her mother, Elisabeth understood that it was important for her daughter's happiness to be able to believe later on that her mother had preferred to have her at her side. She didn't begrudge her daughter this thought.

When Wilbert came home and asked where Coco was, she'd say, 'In her room.' In the period when he was still drinking, he didn't go and look, he just walked straight to the fridge. Sometimes he didn't ask a thing. He didn't seem to notice that when he fucked her Mr. Owl was no longer singing.

But one day he stopped in the kitchen doorway and said, 'I'm not happy.'

'Do you want a beer?' she asked.

'Miriam,' he said—Miriam was the new permanent employee at the shop, she'd taken a lot of work off his hands, an enormous help—'Miriam is worried about my drinking.'

How dare she, Elisabeth thought, how dare she, she doesn't have the right. How dare she, she thought, in a perfect *aaba* scheme.

He didn't drink that evening. They didn't fuck either. He wanted to talk.

WHEN COCO GOES into the hall, she sees her mother sitting halfway up the stairs. A short while ago her mother had said she was going for a lie-down.

'What are you doing?' Coco asks.

'I'm on my way upstairs.'

'Can you manage it?'

'I'm having a little rest.'

Coco leans against the doorpost. 'Crazy, isn't it? Me here.'

'Yes?'

Her mother seems to be panting, as though talking is an effort. Coco considers how to formulate the question, of whether her mother finds it bothersome that she's here. How can she ask it so that she gets an honest answer? Or how can she ask it so that she gets a believable answer? Then her mother coughs, in the way people only do in films to show they are seriously ill and Coco thinks: it doesn't matter whether we enjoy being here together, under a single roof. I'm here because it's necessary. This is a pleasant thought, she must remember it.

'Would it be better if your bed was downstairs?' she asks.

Her mother looks downstairs and says, 'Downstairs is just as far away as upstairs.'

'I'll help you up.'

'I'm all right now.'

Her mother stands up slowly. Coco follows her up the stairs now, like you'd follow a child that wants to go upstairs on its own, ready to catch it. She follows her mother like a shadow, all the way into the bedroom. She lifts up the covers for her. Puts them back over her mother's body without touching it.

'Night-night.'

'Sleep tight,' her mother says.

Coco goes to her own bedroom without thinking. It is three in the afternoon.

Coco lies on the bed. The air in the radiator bubbles so loudly it sounds like a deep fat fryer. Like she is sinking into the oil with the croquettes, that's how heavy her body feels on the mattress.

'Sleep tight, little fish,' her mother used to say to her. Every Wednesday afternoon, her mother would pick her up from school. One night a week she slept at her mother's house, the house where she'd been born. Her mother had started working more, her stepmother less. Everything had been figured out—by Miriam, who was good at figuring things like that out. It was good if the mother—and at the end of the day she is your mother, Miriam said—got to see the child once a week, picked up the child from school, fed the child, put the child to bed, woke up the child, took the child to school. All of this in a clearly defined short space of time. The child experienced the mother, the mother couldn't do much serious damage. Nothing that the father and the stepmother couldn't repair between Thursday afternoon and Wednesday morning.

'It was the best setup for everyone,' Miriam said later.

She was six when one Wednesday afternoon she was sitting at the table with her mother, eating a rusk with brown sugar. For her it was an unusual delicacy. Only years later did she understand that it was a lunch which required no preparation. Rusks and brown sugar, her mother had large stocks of them in the cupboard.

That morning in the playground, one of the older girls had talked about 'the fishwife.' This was a new word. A strange word. Something that fit her mother. Since she was 'the little fish' herself, they must be talking about her mother.

That afternoon she asked her, 'Mum, are you the fishwife?'

Her mother looked at her, astonished, intrigued. She felt she had her attention.

All of a sudden her mother smiled, an overwhelmingly joyous smile and said, 'Yes, I'm the fishwife.'

Coco felt special. The fish and the fishwife. Suddenly they belonged together.

In the evening her mother said, 'Sleep tight, little fish.'

'Good night, fishwife,' the fish said.

On Thursday afternoon, Miriam said that she should never call her mother a fishwife again.

Coco awakes with a start when the doorbell rings. Her mother's slow footsteps echo downstairs on the old, creaky, herringbone parquet. They must have slept for a long time. Coco gets up, goes from her bedroom to the stairs and stops when she hears Hans's voice.

'I've come for Coco.'

'She's upstairs.'

'I'm Hans.'

'Then you're the one with the Mercedes. Matt-grey. You don't see that colour very often.'

Coco hears her mother going back into the sitting room.

'I've come for Coco,' Hans repeats.

Her mother says, 'Yes, so you said, yes.'

Coco sits down on the top step.

'She's upstairs?'

'Will you close the door?'

Her mother's voice sounds further away, presumably she's gone back to sit in her chair at the window.

'If there's a draught and the connecting door upstairs is open,' she says, 'it slams so hard. Sometimes it's the front door that slams, other times it's the door upstairs. There used to be a connecting door downstairs, maybe that's why, you can see it at the neighbours', they've got one of those connecting doors with engraved glass, but that's a rental house. We bought this, my husband and I, a long time ago, though. We paid the equivalent of forty thousand euros for it. Ninety thousand gilders, but that was a lot of money at the time.'

Coco holds her breath and listens. She'd forgotten that her mother could do this too: lose herself in language in the company of strangers, forget the other person. She'd learned to control herself in her daughter's company. Their discomfort had hindered normal speech for so long.

'Now you might say I should have bought the entire street, but no one does that now either, even if you ought to...'

Coco feels how familiar this noise is, her mother's babbling. Something she must have heard a lot as a child.

'My mother always said,' her mother says now, '"A De Wit doesn't rent, a De Wit buys." So when Coco came along, we bought a place. At first we were still looking at renting, but my mother wouldn't have that, so then they bought and we paid them back.'

'We,' her mother says, as though they've been transported back twenty years.

'Coco ought to buy too, but it's not that easy anymore. Of course she'll inherit this house if anything happens to me, it's in my name, Wilbert didn't want anything of it...'

Coco smiles because Hans is standing in the doorway to the sitting room at her mercy, no doubt he has a clear goal in mind, but he has been waylaid by sentences that just won't end.

'Yes,' he says, 'because what would a house like this cost these days?'

'Eight hundred thousand. There was one in the street sold for almost a million recently, but that was a whole house, they didn't have any upstairs neighbours, we do, the top two floors don't belong to us. We've got the basement, the ground floor, and the first floor. We're in a housing corp. with the upstairs neighbours, but actually it doesn't mean much. If we meet once a year that's a lot. We do have a joint account for...'

But Hans soon gets the measure and when she pauses for breath, not even at the end of a sentence, he butts in, 'In her room? Coco is in her room?'

'Yes, in her room. Upstairs,' as though it's only a matter of reminding him where Coco's room is.

'Up the stairs?'

'Yes, if you want to go upstairs you have to use the stairs.'

Hans says, 'I don't know where Coco's room is.'

Then there's silence. Coco rests her head on the banister. She forgets that there are other people there, Coco thinks, that people exist who don't know where the bedrooms are.

But her mother says, ' Of course you don't know where Coco's room is. You've never been here before. You need to turn right at the top of the stairs, and then it's the left-hand bedroom at the front of the house.'

A balding middle-aged man is sitting on her bed in her childhood bedroom. Coco thinks: so this is the man I love. It amazes and amuses her. But of course the man doesn't see himself sitting on the bed in her childhood bedroom and it doesn't amuse him at all. He sits on the edge, his hands in his lap, taking up as little space as possible.

'I thought you didn't want to come here.'

'We have to talk.'

'If people say we have to talk, they've usually come to tell you something.'

'Yes.'

'What do you want to tell me?'

'It's not going well. Us.'

It has come sooner than she'd expected. She becomes alert instantly. No, not instantly. For a brief moment she panics, terrified that he is going to leave her now, now already. The fear is so great she can't bear it. She stays calm, there's no visible shaking, no sign of nerves. But right under the surface of her skin, everything is trembling.

'I think we should stop.'

She says nothing, doesn't move, just looks at him.

'You don't seem surprised,' he says.

With total self-control, she raises an arm and rubs her cheek affectedly. 'I know you have your doubts. I've already said I don't mind.'

'That's the point.'

Don't contradict him anymore. Go along with it now.

'I'm more than halfway through my life, I have my own practice, I have an ex-wife, I'm going bald, I've got a car.'

'You've got a car.'

'It's not about the car.'

'Of course it's not about the car.'

'You don't have your own house.'

'No.'

'You're studying. Or you should be. You have to sort things out with your parents, you have to... you have to .... This whole business with your mother. I've done all that. I'm too old for this. But you have to go through it. You have to make your own mistakes.'

'Mistakes?'

'You have to be able to make them.'

'Is it because I live here now?'

'Please, Coco, I know much more than you! I turn into an intolerable person when I'm around you. I don't want to be like that.'

'You're not like that,' Coco says, much too fast.

'Yes I am, Coco.'

'Yes,' she says and laughs, because this is the man she can say anything to, the first person she can say anything to, and she mustn't lose that. She mustn't lose being-able-to-say-everything, even though it means not being able to say some things to him anymore. Her thoughts jam, but the fact that he can't leave continues to reverberate. He is talking about mistakes she has to make again.

'You have to live,' she hears him say, but she doesn't want to live, she wants *him*. She can't say that aloud either, it would drive him away even faster.

She looks at the arch of his upper lip, its fine contours. The dark eyes that always shine and the nose with its subtle, so regal curves. From a distance he's a balding, somewhat corpulent middle-aged man, but from close up there are those eyes, those lips, those eyebrows, those slender hands. You have to stay close. From close up everything is good and that's what she wants, to be so close to someone that she no longer knows where she ends and he begins. He has stopped talking, the eyes shine more than usual. He is afraid. He can't be alone. That's why she was able to catch him. She knows that now. His divorce wasn't even through.

'You're not an intolerable person. An intolerable person would never call himself intolerable.'

He smiles cautiously. 'I have to let you go,' he says.

'I love you.'

He says, 'I don't respect you.'

Now he's not smiling. He means it. She feels the anger rising inside, but still she remains calm and runs through her options. She won't let him go just like that. She wants to beat him again. No one leaves her, goddammit. She sits down next to him on the bed.

'That's not great,' she says. She lets herself fall back and looks up at him. She smiles. She lays a hand on his thigh, too close to the groin. It doesn't need much, she is young. She is fat, but she is young, it suits her.

'Your mother,' he whispers as she zips open his fly.

'I'm not interested in my mother,' Coco says. She pulls his trousers down over his hips, he works with her, lifting up his buttocks slightly. His cock is hard and erect in his underpants. She pulls his pants off. She kneels down between his legs, spreads his legs. She holds one hand gently against his cock, on the side it bends towards a little. That way it's resting against her hand. She bends over and she licks him slowly from the balls upwards. She licks his cock, very gently and carefully, until it is completely wet. She gently licks across his glans. She bites, with full wet lips, the way you'd bite the top off an ice cream. He trembles. He jerks. She lets saliva drip over his cock, making everything even wetter. She sits up, takes off her trousers, climbs over him and uses one hand to guide his wet cock in the right direction, sits down on him, glides around him and sighs. She goes up, down, tilting her hips backwards and forwards, fucks him, leans back, feels with a hand behind her to grab onto his balls, pushes them against her buttocks. She fucks him and forgets him. He's leaving anyway. She does what she feels like, rides him, disappears.

'I'm...' she says, but she doesn't finish the sentence —I'm dying—don't scare him off, but she is. She feels her eyes turn away, catches just a glimpse of his fearful look. She shakes her head, like someone dismissing an image, she smiles. Then he gets up, still inside her. She rolls over. Now she lies on her back and he thrusts hard into her. She groans.

'Am I hurting you?' he asks.

Instead of, 'Yes, but I want that,' she says, 'No.'

As he fucks her, she feels herself becoming an object and she wants to become an object. Her body slackens and she remembers her old plastic inflatable seal and how she used to lie on top of the animal when it needed emptying and how one afternoon she'd just stayed there lying on it at the bottom of the garden and had fallen asleep. She had woken up, sweating on the flat blue plastic seal in the sun.

'Am I too heavy?' he asks. He's been lying on her without moving for a while.

'No,' she says.

He rolls off her.

'Sometimes you look like you're in pain,' he says. She smiles like one of those dolls with special features. She is changing in her mother's house. It feels familiar, being an object, but she knows he mustn't see it. He kisses the scar on her forehead. He kisses the large scar on her neck, on her back. He kisses the scar on her calf and carries on searching.

'All of them from the sunroom window?' he asks.

'I think so. I don't know, there was always something that was bleeding, wasn't there? When you were a kid your knees were always all scabbed, or your elbows.'

'Not me, I never had scabby knees,' Hans says.

'Then you were a strange child.'

'Because I never walked through a window?'

'Cycled.'

They got dressed. Hans didn't say anything. Coco smiled. It wouldn't be polite, fucking her and then leaving her. More time had been won.

'What are you doing with me?' Hans asks as he ties his shoelaces, panting.

'I'm like a dog from a dog's home,' Coco says, 'eternally grateful.'

He looks up, concerned, his face is red from bending down.

'We'll see,' Coco says, 'OK? I get it.'

'You're a special woman,' he says.

Keeping up the smile is difficult. It doesn't seem good to her, being a special woman.

As she lets Hans out, the framer's van stops in front of the door. Martin's beard has gone grey.

'All right Coco, m'doll! I heard about you.'

'Yes, I'm living here for a while.'

'Yes, that's what she said.'

'Who?'

'Your mother, who else?' Martin says and Coco feels warm, the way being in love feels warm, because her mother mentions her to other people. Martin fetches a rollator from the back of the van.

'This is Martin, Mum's boss,' she says to Hans. They shake hands. Hans doesn't introduce himself.

'I'm on the doubles, could you just chuck this inside?' Martin asks, lifting up the rollator and giving it to Hans. Hans goes back into the house. Her mother's voice, she can't hear what she's saying. Then she hears Hans explaining how the rollator works, that it's got a brake, as though he knows everything about rollators and teaches people how to use them all the time.

'I didn't know she was getting a rollator.'

'Oh, we're looking after her.'

'We're going to put the bed downstairs.'

'Need any help?' Martin gets back in.

'Dad and Miriam are helping.'

'I see. Give my regards to your mother. I'll be back tomorrow, but she knows that.'

Martin leaves. Coco waits for Hans on the pavement. He doesn't appear for a long time. She doesn't hear anything.

When he comes outside, he says, 'I don't mind her.'

'Sorry?'

'Your mother and me, we can get along all right.'

'You're not interested in her,' Coco says.

'Did I say that?'

'Yes.'

'Well, then that's changed.' He chuckles to himself and Coco thinks she ought to laugh too, she doesn't want to be uptight. She doesn't laugh.

'She's got something,' Hans says now, 'and I don't say that about many people.'

'So she should be happy about that? She should consider herself honoured?'

He keeps on chuckling and kisses her, the way you'd kiss a girlfriend you'll see again soon. He finds her mother interesting.

THE HAIRDRESSER HELPS Elizabeth out of her coat. She doesn't move. She lets her arms hang loosely beside her body as he takes off her coat. She's still recovering from the zip. She was trembling so much when she tried to open the coat's zip that she'd barely managed it. She had come on foot. After all she had a rollator now and that's what they're for, isn't it? So you can keep on walking. Why'd you get so bloody tired then? She'd only called yesterday but he had space today.

'Wash and set,' she says as she sits down. She'd had it cut recently.

'Wash and set?'

It was a thing for old ladies. She has often seen him do it. Some of them came every week. Which is not that odd, with a wash and set.

'Just giving it a try.'

'So that's what we'll do.'

'Did you hear about my daughter?'

'What?'

'Living with me again.'

'You're kidding.'

'Her idea.'

'Not managing anymore on your own then?'

'She wants to spend a bit more time with me, she said.'

'Is it difficult for her?'

'What?'

'You being sick.'

'For her?'

'You are her mother.'

'Yes, that's true I suppose.'

'Really nothing off?'

'Just a wash and set.'

'Hope it doesn't rain.'

'Otherwise I'll just stay here.'

'I've got enough reading material.'

'Exactly.'

'She's not any easy child.'

'Nervous type. Always has been.'

When Elisabeth sits under the hood dryer she feels how calm she is. Wilbert is coming this afternoon. Of course. Now that he's needed. He comes when he's needed. The bed has to go downstairs. Miriam is coming with him. Coco told her this morning, she looked anxious. How nervous that child is. I have to help people a bit, Elisabeth thinks. I have to show them that everything's fine. They don't know that.

The first time she saw Miriam, Wilbert and Coco had already moved out. It was a Thursday and Coco was at school. The toy rabbit that should have gone with her in her rucksack had been left behind. Coco couldn't do without the rabbit. Elisabeth went to the shop to drop it off.

When she entered the shop and saw the little dumpy woman behind the counter, Elisabeth smiled. Ach, she thought, it's only you, as if she already knew her.

'You're Miriam,' she said.

'Yes,' Miriam said.

Elisabeth held up the fluffy rabbit.

'Elisabeth,' Miriam said.

'Coco's rabbit,' Elisabeth said.

'Och, the raaabbit,' Miriam said, she had a Groningen accent.

Elisabeth smiled again. It was fine. He could live with this dumpy little woman. The phone rang. Miriam turned around, she had a flat arse. Her plumpness was a width thing only. Big hips, no arse. Elisabeth knew that she was better and silently gave them permission. It didn't matter. The woman didn't matter.

The hairdresser turns off the hood dryer and feels her hair.

'Just a bit more,' he says.

'You've never met her, have you?'

'Who?'

'Wilbert's new wife.'

'No,' the hairdressers says, 'quite a simple woman I hear.'

'Yes,' Elisabeth says, 'a sweet woman, you know, a really sweet woman.'

'Yes, I suppose. Another five minutes.' He turns the dryer back on.

The hairdresser helps her into her coat and this time he does the zip.

'Come here, Liz,' he says and kisses her three times on the cheeks. It's the first time he has kissed her. He turns around at once, to open the door for her.

She wants to walk to the frame shop, but she is too tired. When she finally makes it home and stands in her own hall, the shaking has become so bad that she can no longer open the coat zip. She sits down on her rollator. The bell rings. Coco runs down the stairs and falters when she sees her.

'Oh... You're back already.'

Elisabeth doesn't know what that 'oh' means, apart from that it always means something and she's too tired to decode it.

'Can you open the door?' she asks.

'Dad's coming to help with the bed.'

'Yes, I know that. Can you just open it?'

Coco goes around her and waits by the door.

'And Miriam too.' The bell goes again.

'Come on, just open it.'

Coco opens the door, slowly. Elisabeth sees Wilbert, just Wilbert. Ach, of course, no different from usual. She always sees him on Coco's birthday, but he never comes to the house anymore. Miriam is standing behind him. Wilbert kisses his daughter and comes into the hall. Elisabeth smiles at him.

'Oh, were you just leaving?' he asks.

'I just got in,' she said. 'I've still got my coat on. Could you help me with the zip? I can't get the zip open.'

Wilbert gives her a funny look. They all give her a funny look.

'I'm shaking, so I can't get the zip open.'

Wilbert doesn't react.

'The zip just needs opening,' she says, 'that's all.'

'I'll help you,' Coco says.

Wilbert immediately steps to the side and Coco helps her take her coat off. Miriam is still standing in the porch. She doesn't budge. Everyone looks at her now. Why are they doing that? It must be annoying.

'Look at you,' says Elisabeth.

'Yes,' says Miriam, 'it's me.'

'Older, aren't you.' Elisabeth says.

'Pardon?'

'You're older.'

'Mum!' What's this now?

'Aren't we all?'

'We all are, Coco, we all are!' Miriam smiles. She doesn't need to. 'I came along too, I hope you don't mind. Wilbert asked me to help with the bed. I thought it would be all right.' Now she smiles like someone in pain, but she doesn't move an inch.

'Didn't you have to be in the shop?'

'I stopped working in the shop ages ago.'

'Mum, you know that.'

'I work from home,' Miriam says.

'Are you coming in?'

'Yes?'

Hadn't she been clear? 'You're not a vampire, are you?'

'Mum!'

'Because vampires can't enter a house until they've been invited.' She says it fast. Just to explain. 'That's why.'

'Mum!'

'What?'

'Stop being weird.'

'I'm not saying she's a vampire. You didn't take it like that, did you, Miriam?'

'No, of course not.'

'Come in,' Coco says, and only then does Miriam come into the hall.

'Didn't you know that?' Elisabeth doesn't want to be misunderstood. 'You have to be invited in by someone who actually lives in the house. If you're a vampire.'

'I actually live in this house, don't I?' says Coco.

Elisabeth thinks: that's not true and says, 'It doesn't really matter whether you do or not because Miriam isn't a vampire. Are you, Miriam?'

'Not that I know of.' Miriam giggles.

'I'm sure you like some coffee?' Be friendly. Be obviously friendly. Even towards her. 'Miriam too? Come on, no, to the right, we always sit in the kitchen. Don't we? Wilbert?'

'Where does the bed need to go?' Wilbert asks. 'Shall

we do the bed first?' He goes into the sitting room. Coco and her mother follow him.

The liar. As though he doesn't know her. As though they didn't always sit in the kitchen. As though all those years they've no longer been together weren't just nonsense, as though they couldn't pick up where they left off. In three days you can make a frame five centuries old, in two hours you can make it new. Time is nothing.

Elisabeth stands on the doorstep, leaning on her rollator.

Miriam says, 'Of course Coco has filled us in a little bit on the whole state of affairs and all that.'

Elisabeth is curious as to what 'little bit on the whole state of affairs' Coco has filled her in on, but she doesn't want to be difficult. She sees their discomfort. She says, 'That's good.'

'It's shit,' Wilbert says.

'Yes,' Elisabeth says.

'The bed,' Coco says.

Elisabeth steps to the side, Coco and Miriam go up the stairs. Wilbert pauses in the hall. He waits until Coco and Miriam can no longer hear him.

'Are you all right?' he asks.

'I'm all right,' Elisabeth says. Wilbert shaved yesterday but not today. She can still see from his beard growth how many days ago it was. She feels it in the palm of her hand. She knows how it would feel were she to lay her hand on his cheek.

THE BED IS going in the sunroom, under the old chandelier in front of the large window that takes up the entire back wall. The sofa is at right angles to the bed. It fits if the sunroom doors are left open. Coco stands next to the bed and looks into the garden, which is a few metres lower. The basement is no longer in use. She tries to make out the crack in gravel tiles of the terrace where she fell, but the tiles are green and muddy and the crack is covered.

Coco waits until her father and Miriam have finished saying goodbye to her mother. She wants them to leave, but they don't. She hears her mother call out something about coffee again.

Coco reluctantly goes into the small kitchen.

Her father knocks on the radiator and says, 'You need to get the air out of this.'

Her mother says, 'Or would you rather have tea, Miriam?'

Miriam says, 'I just wanted to say: I think it's really awful for you, with the illness and everything. If we can do anything to help, it goes without saying that we will.'

Coco feels sick. You can't mix everything, she thinks. Some things really don't taste good together.

'So it's coffee then,' her mother says.

'Not for me,' says Coco.

'Lovely.' Miriam sits down.

'You can both go now if you want,' Coco says. 'It's just the bed business I couldn't do on my own and Hans is busy at work. Really great that you could help, but you can go now if you want, you know. Martin's coming in a bit too.'

'She wants coffee,' her mother says.

'If it's no trouble,' Miriam says.

'Do you want coffee or not?'

'Aren't you having any?'

'Trouble with my stomach.' Her father goes into the sitting room.

'He's restless,' her mother says, 'he always was. Coco, do you want coffee too?'

Coco wants to get out of the kitchen, wait until her father comes back, sorts it out. Her father doesn't come back.

Her father is sitting on the bed.

'Is that all right,' Coco asks, 'the two of them alone?'

Her father says, 'Miriam is very good with people.'

'You're relaxed.'

'They're adults.'

'Is she really going to stay for a coffee?'

'I think so.'

'I don't think I've ever seen them for so long together.'

'On your birthday?'

'That's different, more people. This is... this is... a Barbie and a Sindy.'

'A Barbie and a Sindy?'

'I used to have Barbies but also a Sindy. Sindy had a much bigger head. If you saw Sindy on her own it wasn't that strange, but with Barbie next to her that head suddenly looked really crazy, and Barbie's head much too small. It's a bit like that with Mum and Miriam. When they're on their own, they're not that strange, but together...'

Her father laughs.

'Don't you think?'

'Great for Hans,' he said, 'that conference in Seattle?'

'What do you mean?'

'That he'll be the keynote speaker, that's pretty special.'

'He's what?'

'Keynote speaker. Right? I bumped into him yesterday in Hoogstins Bookshop, he was having coffee with Eelke. Cool, isn't it?'

'What?'

'Being keynote speaker.'

'Yes.'

'Didn't you know?'

'I'm not sure... whether I knew.' She is alarmed. The sudden realisation that she should have known hits her. Hans has been talking about the conference for months, but his words were elusive, like when her father talked about turnover. Each day he'd announce what had been sold, whether the result had been good or disappointing.

She'd learned to smile at the right moment like her stepmother and say, 'Oh really?' whenever he'd sold two espresso machines in a single day.

She thinks of the times Hans had talked about the conference and wonders whether she'd said, 'Oh really?' too.

'NOTHING IS AS nice as fresh sheets,' Coco says as she pulls the fitted sheet over the mattress. Elisabeth doesn't say that she should have put on an underlay first.

She is sitting on the sofa next to the bed, looking at her daughter as though she's five years old again and wants to help fold the wash but only makes it worse by helping.

'Do you know that Dad said you locked me up in my bedroom when I wasn't even eighteen months old?'

Elisabeth hears her daughter's attempt to sound breezy. So she replies just as breezily, 'Did he say that?'

'Yes, he said that.'

'That father of yours.' She does her best to fit in with Coco, over and over. The previous evening she'd even tried to eat more, if only to show her that they weren't that different after all, though she knows otherwise.

'It's not true is it?' Her daughter looks at her.

She doesn't reply fast enough. Now there's no going back. 'Your father wouldn't make a thing like that up. Why would your father make up something like that?'

'You locked me up?'

'Do you remember anything of it?'

'So it's true?'

'But can you remember it?'

'Mum, you locked me up when I was a year and half?'

'Times were different, you know,' Elisabeth says, trying to sound like the hairdresser.

'You don't lock up a one-and-a-half-year-old child.'

'You didn't cry any louder when you were in your room. You really didn't. It didn't make any difference.'

'A year and a half?'

'Would you pass me that plastic bag?' She points under the bed. Coco bends down and gives her the bag from the chemist's.

'A year and a half?' she repeats.

Elisabeth gets the morphine plasters out of the bag and puts them next to the sofa.

'Did Dad say a year and a half?'

'You mean he's lying?'

'Lying? How do you figure that one out?'

'You're avoiding the subject.'

'Am I?' She unfolds the information leaflet.

'Yes, you are. Can't you do that later?'

'Oh sorry, is it bothering you?'

'Yes.'

Elisabeth puts everything back in the bag.

'The pain's not that bad really. Methinks.'

'What?'

'Methinks.'

Her daughter looks at the bag.

'Well, put it back.' She gives her daughter the bag. 'Then we can have a nice chat. Just ask me, I don't have any secrets. What do you want to know?'

'Why would you lock up a child of a year and a half?'

Elisabeth wants to give her an honest answer, but her thoughts have already digressed. 'A playpen is a kind of lock-up too, isn't it?'

'Mum, I asked you something.'

'You need to put an underlay on.'

'Huh?'

'You need to put on an underlay underneath the fitted sheet. Yes, I'm just being honest. You want me to be honest, don't you?'

'Why did you lock me up?'

Elisabeth searches for something true she is happy to share. She has a good memory. She says, 'I put cushions down everywhere. In your room. All the cushions from the sofa and the big ones from the old easy chairs. I used belts to tie cushions to the corners of the cupboards so that you couldn't bump yourself. I left you three bottles. Two with water and one with freshly-squeezed orange juice. You liked that. I broke up biscuits into small pieces and put them in plastic bags. At the time you didn't eat well unless you could get the food out of small plastic bags yourself. You liked that.'

Her daughter doesn't say anything.

'And there were toys,' Elisabeth says, 'cardboard cubes, from big to small, that fit inside each other. A wooden lighthouse with coloured rings. A book with animals that made sounds. A big cow that mooed when you pressed her belly.'

'How long did you leave me there?'

Elisabeth looks at the paler strands in her girl's hair and then her eyes descend to the fleshy neck.

'I liked to kiss your neck,' she says. 'My face fit perfectly into the space between your throat and your shoulders. You smelt so lovely as a child.' They don't know that you love them, you have to tell them. Again and again. *'I love you.* That's what I'd say when I tucked you in at night. *Bye-bye, little girl. I love you.'* Elisabeth's gaze wanders off. She looks out of the window and thinks about the matt-grey Mercedes. Then her daughter tears the sheet from the bed.

'Are you angry now?'

'Why would I be angry? You have to put an underlay on, don't you. Explain it to me, Mum, why would I be angry?'

'Because I locked you up. You're angry because I locked you up, aren't you?'

'Yes, don't you think?'

'You weren't at the time. Not at the time, you know. You were angry when I didn't lock you up too. You were always angry. It didn't make any difference.'

'And you blamed a child of one-and-a-half for that?'

'No, darling, you don't have to feel guilty about it— you couldn't help it.'

'I don't feel guilty!' Coco says. 'What do you expect?!'

Elisabeth has that strange feeling in her chest again. Perhaps it's indigestion. Her daughter walks away, out of the room.

'What is it now?'

'I'm fetching an underlay!'

She hears the heavy footsteps in the corridor, on the stairs, the landing. The creaking doors of the big old linen cupboard upstairs. On the inside of the cupboard door there's half a Donald Duck sticker. Coco stuck it there a long time ago. Elisabeth tried to get it off, but his legs and part of his tail wouldn't come off. There's a bit of paint missing where his body used to be. Footsteps descending. Coco seems calmer when she comes back into the room. She makes the bed in silence and then sits down on it. Her girl runs a hand through her hair.

'Are you growing your hair out?'

'It's just been cut.'

'Oh, that's it then, I knew there was something different.'

'I should be studying.'

...

'I said: I should be studying.'

'What's that got to do with your hair?'

'I'm not talking about my hair. I'd like to have my desk here.'

'Of course,' she says, 'your desk here,' because now she

wants to understand everything for a while. She is already nodding.

'Do you think I could borrow Martin's van?'

'Yes,' she says, because you can always borrow Martin's van and he's so helpful and Elisabeth says what her daughter wants to hear: 'Do you want his number?' and even, 'Or should I call him for you?'

Something went wrong between her and Wilbert after Coco's birth and now everything is over and Wilbert has gone and Coco is here. Wilbert started giving her funny looks and Coco gave her looks like that too, later. She only got strange when she became a mother and she knows she can't blame the child, although the reason she can't seems harder and harder to grasp and she already regrets that Coco's desk is coming here.

'IT TURNED INTO a bit more,' Coco says. The desk is in the hall. Boxes and bags are waiting on the pavement. Martin is looking for somewhere to park the van.

'Yes,' her mother says.

'We were driving anyway.'

'Yes, now you have the van...'

'... it'd be a shame not to use it.' Her mother looks at the bin bag in her hand.

'Clothes,' she says.

'Clothes,' her mother repeats.

'I'll take some of it up now.' She carries the bin bag up the stairs, turns around on the second step, 'Can I bring anything downstairs for you?'

'For me?'

'Things you want downstairs. Since I'm going anyway.'

'Yes, you might as well...'

'Now I'm going anyway.' Her mother keeps her gaze focussed on the bin bag in her arms. Coco would rather her mother didn't watch her bring everything in and says, 'Go and sit down, go on.'

'Yes,' her mother says, 'I'll have a nice lie-down.'

Coco hears that the word 'nice' isn't her mother's word.

The desk is on the landing. Martin and Coco pause to catch their breath.

'Is it going to fit in your bedroom?' Martin asks.

'Tight.' The door to her mother's bedroom is open. It's the biggest and prettiest bedroom on the first floor. It is empty without her bed. They both look in. Coco waits.

'Just say the word,' Martin says. 'Where do you want it?' Coco waits.

'Next to your bed?'

'Not much room.'

'Yes.'

'What now?'

'Just say the word.'

'Let's put it in Mum's room for a while,' Coco says, 'then we'll see about it later.' They carry the desk in.

'How's business?' Coco asks.

'It's a bit of a slog without your mother.'

'Busy?'

'She's actually the only one who can do the gilding,' Martin says. 'She was teaching the others, but no one is as good as her.'

'She's not your normal woman.'

'The best framer in the city, that's what she is.'

'She's not easy either, obviously.'

'Don't believe she ever took a day off sick.'

'Dad always used to get furious when she said: "They're happy with me at my work." She'd say that.'

'And we are.'

'"No one at work has a problem with me", she'd say.'

'We never have had either.'

'She was the one to tell me how they'd argue. I don't remember it anymore. But then he'd say she wasn't right in her head and then she'd say it again: "No one at work has a problem with me".'

'No, never.'

'Craftswoman, of course.'

'And patient with people. Never lost it with any of the interns. Very good teacher.'

'Teacher?'

'Do you want coffee?' her mother shouted from downstairs. Martin was already walking away.

Martin is sitting on the edge of her mother's bed. They are talking about their work, using words that Coco doesn't know. Pretty words. Rabbit-skin glue. Champagne chalk. It's as though she can smell the framer's shop, which she visited just once or twice only as a child. Just like normal people, Coco thinks.

'You don't have to see me out, stay in bed.' Martin hugs her. It doesn't look unnatural, though Coco is sure she's never seen her mother hugging anyone before.

'I'd like to come back, once all this business...' Her mother makes a dismissive gesture along her upper arm where a morphine plaster has been applied. 'I'd like to come back. It would be all right if my hands didn't shake so much. If I could sit down.'

'Is there any post I should take for you?' Martin asks.

'Coco,' her mother says, 'could you fetch that pile of papers from the dresser?'

Coco gets the post. In her haste she sees envelopes from official bodies, insurance company, social services, but also a postcard. 'Thinking of you. Hans and Janine.' The neighbours.

She waits for her mother to sort the post into administrative and personal matters, but she says, 'Do you want a bag or is it all right like this?' Martin takes the whole pile and glances at it. He reads the postcard unabashedly.

Her mother's post disappears into the grubby canvas bag he always has with him. The postcard too.

'You do a lot for Mum,' Coco says.

'All the paperwork is for Martin,' her mother says.

Coco thinks about the postcards she used to send to her mother when she was a child. 'A postcard isn't paperwork, though, is it?' she says, 'That's something different from admin. Mum, you can't get someone else to handle your private life.'

Her mother gives her a lengthy look, as though she hasn't understood her, but then she says, 'Martin should know which people have shown interest, for the funeral, if he's going to be the one organising it.'

'Funeral.'

'Martin always takes care of everything. Don't you worry.'

ELISABETH'S HANDS ARE resting on her stomach. She feels every vibration under her skin. The hands rest there with the same expectation as during her pregnancy— that movement is on its way, that the child will swim towards the hands, that it will turn there, twist, push, roll. Movements that get stronger every day. But later, when the child was supposed to be somewhere else, the hands stayed there and there was always a vibration, a shudder, movement. The child had never gone away. Elisabeth closes her eyes and feels the miniscule movements underneath her fingers. Then a bang. Something falls upstairs. She hears Coco swearing.

'Stay away,' Elisabeth whispers. Upstairs something large is pushed across the floor. Elisabeth sits up. Will come in a minute. Will want to talk. She hears a door and she is already sighing, that will be her. No footsteps follow.

I just want to lie down for a bit. Can't a person just lie down? It's quiet again now. What is she up to? Elisabeth throws off the covers, sits on the edge of the bed.

Will need coffee for sure. What a lot of coffee that child drinks. Everything runs out quicker with her in the house. Where has she got to?

Elisabeth struggles to her feet and grips the rollator. She rolls it across the room, lifts it over the doorstep, goes along the hall, listens from the bottom of the stairs.

'Coco?' No reply.

'Coco?' Again nothing. She must realise it's tiring, that shouting.

'Coco?!' Does she want coffee or not? It's much too cold in the hall.

'Cooocooo?!' Finally a door and footsteps.

'Yes, what is it?' Coco stands at the top of the stairs.

'Do you want coffee or not?'

'Coffee?'

'Is it such a difficult question?'

'Have you already put it on?'

'What do you mean?'

'Are you putting coffee on?'

'If you want coffee.'

'Do you want to have coffee...? Together?'

'Do *you* want coffee?'

'I'd be happy to have some coffee, but I'm studying. But if you already have some or you're putting some on...'

'Well, then I'll put some on, if you want coffee.' Elisabeth sighs, turns her rollator, and goes to the kitchen.

'What's the matter now?' Coco calls after her.

'I'm just not used to it,' Elisabeth calls back as she enters the kitchen, 'having to make coffee for someone else all day again. I drink two cups in the morning, myself.'

Coco comes stomping downstairs, walks past her into the kitchen. 'You're the one who suggested coffee!'

Elisabeth fills the kettle. Puts the full kettle onto the rollator and wants to walk to the other end of the counter with it. The water sloshes out.

'Can't you just put the coffee on? It'll be much quicker.'

'If you want coffee, Mum, you can just ask for it, you know. I'm more than happy to make coffee for you.'

'No thanks, I don't drink coffee in the afternoon.' Coco stares at her, the kettle in her hands. Dark look. Away with her, away. Don't ask, don't try to understand what it is this time. 'What?' she shouldn't have asked. Leave it, leave it. Let it go.

'I was studying.'

'Yes, and I was having a lovely rest in my bed. I don't mind being on my own.'

'Luckily. I'll leave the coffee then, I have to cut down anyway. I'll go back upstairs.'

Elisabeth experiences panic at the thought of Coco going back upstairs. As though Coco is cycling on the other side of the Overtoom again and there's constantly something wrong. Away with this, with this wrongness, this unseemliness. But Coco goes out of the kitchen, and each step she takes away from her she makes everything more unseemly and because 'go away' isn't possible, because 'disappear, don't exist,' isn't an option for a mother, she uses words she finds ugly, Wilbert-words, Coco-words. She's already in the hall.

'Maybe it's not working.' The footsteps stop. The child understands these words. 'Maybe it's not working, Coco.' Coco comes back, her expression different now. Elisabeth sits down on her rollator. Onwards now. Coco back in the kitchen. 'It doesn't matter if you can't cope with me. Martin wouldn't mind helping you move back out. I've already asked him.'

'*What* have you already asked him?'

'That, when, as soon as—that he...'

'You want me to leave?'

'I want you to be happy.' This is true. One of the things. One of the true things. Oneofthethings oneofthethings ofthethings.

Coco sits down at the kitchen table and says, 'I *want* to be here.'

Buffer. The wooden buffer for the toy train. That's what Coco's sentence is like.

A bigger buffer now. 'I want you to go.' It has been said. It's done. Don't fight it. Failure. Now wait for the words, everything passes. Just let the story become: *Things were never resolved between the mother and daughter.*

Coco stays calm.

'Go.' Her daughter will shout in the end.

Silence still. Come on.

'I don't have anywhere to live right now.'

What is happening? Where is the shouting, the wailing, the stamping?

'I don't have anywhere to live right now.'

'Yes, that's what you said.'

'My room. I had to move out.'

'You have to move out?'

'I'm already out. I already had to leave. I told you, didn't I? That I had to move out?'

Tumbling. Elisabeth scarcely knows what is tumbling, only that it's tumbling. There are always abstract constructions of thoughts that she thought didn't exist, but which suddenly can tumble and therefore do exist. Now her daughter's dedication collapses and tumbles.

'I did tell you, though,' her daughter says.

Elisabeth can only nod along now and replies, 'Yes, you said that... on the Overtoom.' Because she does have a good memory. It's just she should have thought more, made connections. It's her own fault.

'Where are all your things?'

'I don't have that much.'

'And when did that all happen?' Elisabeth asks, and she remembers similar sentences from years ago: *And when did you see her then? And how long has it been going on?*

'Does it matter?' her daughter asks.

'That's what your father said too,' Elisabeth says.

'Huh?'

'"Does it matter?"... "It's not about the other person. It's about what we have. Or don't anymore."'

'What are you going on about now?'

'Oh, that whole business, back then.'

'The divorce, you mean.'

'Yes, that whole business with Miriam.'

'Was he already seeing her then?'

'That doesn't matter. It wasn't about that.'

'Christ, Mum, you split up ages ago.'

'Yes.'

'Christ.'

'So you had to move out, but... it doesn't matter.'

'I had to move out, yes.'

'And you wanted to be with me.'

'Yes.'

'And you had to move out.'

'Yes.'

'But you also wanted... really did... to be with me. That's what you wanted.'

'I could have moved back in with Dad.'

'And Miriam's massage parlour then?'

'You mean the shiatsu practice.'

She waits and then asks, 'Is it working out for her?' Coco says nothing. Ask again is the rule, to prove that she's genuinely interested. Ask again, otherwise you prove to them that you're not interested at all. That you have a good memory, but can't remember the word 'shiatsu' because you don't want to remember it. Too tired. Tumble then. Let all the interest drop too. She gets up, the question still hanging in the air: Is it working out for her?

'I'm going for a lie-down.' Rollator. Past the daughter. Don't touch her.

'What's the matter now?' her daughter calls after her.

'Very tired!' is true. Very tired. Back to bed with her hands on her stomach, let the child swim. The little fish in her.

COCO CALLS THE hairdresser and asks him whether he wouldn't mind coming to the house just this once. She knows how much her mother likes seeing him. It's a gift.

She didn't lie about her lodgings. She runs through all the words that have passed between her and her mother and is sure she hasn't lied. Yet she still wants to give her mother a gift, like someone who wants to make up for something.

'I don't actually do that,' the hairdresser says, 'home cuts.'

'She's dying,' Coco says. Everything to persuade the hairdresser. The hairdresser hesitates.

She says, 'It might be the last time,' and feels the warmth rising to her cheeks. Bloody hell, wash and set, she has her hair set these days and likes to go to the hairdresser's once a week. No way that she's going to die within the next seven days.

'Fine,' the hairdresser says.

After that she calls Martin and says that her mother can hardly be left alone anymore. She's declining fast. The more she talks, the more it sounds like the truth and Coco begins to cry automatically and then she asks him, 'It's really true, isn't it? She's not doing well, is she?'

Then she calls Hans.

'Mum's not doing well.'

'Poor sweetheart.'

'It looks like I should stay here for the time being. No other option.'

'Have you already spoken to her GP?'

'He's coming this week, I think.'

'Then you'll know more.'

'When will I see you?'

He doesn't reply at once. 'Nothing has changed,' he says.

'I know.'

'Yes?'

'You've stopped believing in it.'

'Yes.'

'So you don't want to see me anymore?'

'Of course I want to see you.'

'But?'

'I just don't think I can do that to you. I have to let you go.'

'Do you want that?'

'No, but...'

'Let me decide. I'll decide myself what you can do to me or not? OK?... Please?'

'Yes.'

'Fine.'

'There's an exhibition in Haarlem I'd like to see. Sculpture.'

'Then we'll go to the exhibition in Haarlem,' Coco says. 'Can you make tomorrow?'

When she hangs up, she's delighted.

Coco sings a Russian song during the cooking. She stamps along, and when she is waiting for the water to boil for the rice she even claps her hands. Her good mood lasts for a long time, even as she eats with her mother. It isn't until she's lying in bed thinking about the next day that she realises that she doesn't want to go to a sculpture exhibition at all and then falls asleep angry anyway, thinking: that's clever, that I can do that, be angry *and* fall asleep.

ELISABETH GIVES THE taxi driver the address of the framer's and sighs, relieved, as though she's done now— this is the final journey. She allows herself the fleeting thought: I never have to go back after this. This is how she observes the houses in her street one more time as they drive past. She crosses over at the junction one last time, turns into the narrow street with the shop for the last time.

The car stops in front of the glass façade. The taxi driver helps her to get out. Marlie is standing at the computer and looks up. She waves, much too enthusiastically. That's how you wave to people who don't come often, not to a colleague, not to someone who simply belongs there.

As she goes into the shop, her colleagues throng around her. They block the route to her table and greet her at length.

She doesn't look at them, she tries to see past them and says, 'I want to go to my table.' Martin gets a stool and puts it at her table. She sits down, knows that she never sat here but always stood, closes her eyes, and feels for the tools hanging from the corner of her table. She can find her things blindfold. Hammer, present. Pincers, present. Wiper. The wiper has gone. She opens her eyes.

'Who's got my wiper?'

'Which one was yours?' Marlie asks.

'The one with "only for table" on it. It's supposed to be hanging here.' She feels tears. Her wiper has gone. Frans, who should be standing at the back at the cutting machine, brings her her box.

'Isn't it in here?' he asks.

'Put it back,' Elisabeth says. They are only going to bloody give her the box of tools, the way you give things to people who aren't coming back.

'Have a quick look.' Frans goes to put the box on the table.

'Put it back.'

'Don't want a look?' He puts it on the table.

'PUT THAT BOX BACK.' They don't know her like this. She doesn't know herself like this.

'Put that box back right away!' No one moves for a second. She isn't going to smile now, for god's sake don't smile. Don't make amends, there's nothing to amend here, not here, please not here. Twenty years and no one has found her strange here. For twenty years she didn't have to think about how she should relate to others here. Twenty years and everything is still going to be ruined. When Martin gives her his hanky, she realises that she's crying. Frans puts the box back on the shelf and finally goes back to the cutting machine to the rear of the shop.

Please let someone turn on a machine. As though her thoughts have been heard, she hears the underpinner start up. Chack. Chack. Carry on now, just these sounds.

Martin gets a golden frame. He puts it around a colourful painting of flowers on her table.

'What do you think?' he asks. 'Is the inside edge still too fussy or should we leave it as it is?'

'Do you think I'm mad?' Elisabeth asks. For twenty years her eye had been important, now his question was to reassure her. Martin doesn't reply.

'Do you think I'm mad?' She gives him back his haky. The whole shop, which had consisted of the right materials, the right smells, and the right sounds has become a morass of people. Intentions and thoughts have been let in. The shop is leaking. If she stays sitting here for a while there's a chance clients will come in too. How can she get away without drama? How can she flee without being seen? Give it up. The shop is broken. She lets herself sink from the stool, quaking. Martin catches her just in time.

'I have to go.'

'I'll take you,' Martin says, 'wait here, I'll fetch the van.' He helps her back onto the stool. She closes her eyes and lets her head hang.

'Everything is lost,' she says. She remembers Wilbert saying that at the end of every drunken evening: everything is lost. And how pretty those big words were and how lovely that she didn't know what they meant, but all she had to do was support him on his way to bed and undress him and repeat, 'It doesn't matter, it doesn't matter,' and she only had to lie down next to him. Everything is lost. She didn't know at the time that he was unhappy, that it felt like this, like now, like this.

In the evening she falls over. All of a sudden her legs stop working. When she's lying down she's peaceful, but Coco soon finds her, in front of the toilet door.

'If I hadn't been here,' Coco begins, 'you would have died there in the night.'

'Bloody hell, yes,' she says.

COCO IS ON her way back from the chemist's. Hans's Mercedes is there already. He's early. Coco hurries inside as though she has to save him from her mother, but she hears him laughing. She stops in front of the door and listens.

'... so you don't recognise yourself in the description of a person with autism?' Coco becomes angry, until she hears her mother answering him in a reasonable, calm tone of voice.

'I don't have any trouble putting myself in someone else's shoes.'

'You don't think so?'

'You don't think so either, do you?'

'That's a good one.' Hans laughs loudly.

My explicit boyfriend, Coco thinks. Why doesn't she ever ask her mother questions like that? All of a sudden it seems so simple, put that way.

'You have a good memory?'

'Exceedingly.'

'Can I ask about your childhood?'

'What do you want to know?'

Fucking hell, Coco thinks, he is treating her like a client. They jump when she opens the door. She likes that. She's jealous. She doesn't yet know of whom.

'Coco, there aren't very many of them, I was right,' her mother says, 'cars in that colour grey. I always say that, don't I, that it's such a nice colour, his car. And then you act as though I've said something strange, or as though I'm avoiding something, or whatever, as if I've just started talking about the paint instead, but it really is an unusual shade.'

'I was just saying to your mother that she has an unusual relationship to matter and that I'd like to interview her about that.'

'Interview?'

'I'm writing an article about anthropomorphism.'

'For Seattle.'

'Seattle's about neuroses.'

'... Maybe there's... an overlap...'

'I've already finished my Seattle speech.'

'Seattle?' her mother asks.

'Conference,' Hans says.

'Yes,' Coco says, 'he's the keynote speaker.'

'Is that true?' her mother says.

'Are you interested?' Hans seems pleased.

'Mum has to rest,' Coco says.

Hans stands up. 'I'll call you,' he says to her mother, 'will you manage on your own?'

'Martin will be here in an hour,' Coco says.

When she's sitting next to him in the car, she says, 'What you're doing is too intimate.'

She expects him to be shocked, but he just says calmly, 'Yes, funny isn't it, that it feels like that? I do understand, you know. You don't have to feel embarrassed.'

'*I'm* not, no.'

'Oh, *me*? I'm supposed to be embarrassed, you mean?'

She doesn't reply. He doesn't ask for a reply. He finds his own question absurd.

'Do you ever feel embarrassed?' she asks him.

'Embarrassment isn't one of my talents,' he says.

'No.'

'I can't deny it, your mother and me, there is a spark.'

'Unusual.'

'Yes, it is.'

'Hey, if it's really important to you, I'll keep my distance. If it's really important to you, you just have to say so.' Coco still doesn't dare play her trump card.

She places her hand on his leg, moves the hand slowly to his crotch. Everything is soft there. She rubs, squeezes gently. Nothing happens.

'We need to get petrol,' he says.

Coco thinks about Caramac. 'Are you starving already too?'

'Not in the slightest.'

ELISABETH SLEEPS MORE and more. When she opens her eyes, Wilbert has suddenly appeared, on the sofa next to her bed.

'What are you doing here?'

'Coco and Martin made up a roster, so you don't have to be alone anymore.'

'She hates me.'

'What are you saying?'

'... so that I'll never be alone.'

'She said you fell.'

'Yes, so what?'

'She's worried.'

'Revenge is sweet.'

'Try and be normal.'

'Did she just let you leave?'

'Miriam's never been difficult about you.'

'Well.'

'Are you annoyed that I'm here?'

'No.' Her head is still, it feels heavy. She tries to look at Wilbert, see his eyes, but Wilbert keeps looking away. 'You told Coco that I locked her up.'

'Did she bring it up?'

'Yes.'

'Well, yeah, it was true.'

'She didn't remember it.'

'No.'

'And now she does.'

'And that's my fault?'

'Yes.'

'I didn't lock her up, did I?'

'What's she supposed to do with it?'

'Not still trying for Mother of the Year, are you?'

'I'm talking about Coco.'

'Oh, a parenting discussion. Not our forte.'

'*Our*,' she says quietly.

'Sorry,' he says then, 'I don't want to be a jerk, maybe it wasn't so clever of me.'

'We used to have it good, once, didn't we? Before Coco?'

'Yes, that too.'

'That too?'

'We were good too.'

'I've never told you this before,' she says, 'but do you know I always used to think, as far back as school, that you smelled of pencil shavings?'

'You have said that before.'

'Have I said that?'

'Several times.'

'Yes.'

Wilbert takes off his jumper. He is wearing a polo shirt underneath. He has got fat.

'I want to say it again,' Elisabeth says.

'What?'

'I thought you smelled of pencil shavings. But I like that smell. Have I already said that too?'

'Yes, you said that too.'

'Then I might have a good memory, but...'

'Not for the things you say yourself.'

'I always forget whether I've thought something or said it out loud.'

'No, you always forget to look for a reaction. That's it.' His face is angry.

'Oh,' she says, 'is that it?'

'Yes, that's it.'

She lapses into silence.

'What are you thinking about now?' Wilbert asks.

'Things I've already said.'

'Sorry,' he says, 'just say it then.'

She holds out her hand. 'I can still feel it. The finger you put a plaster around, on your sixteenth birthday. I sliced it open on a tin. You put it on very tight. That's when I decided that you were the one for me.'

'Yes.'

'But I'm certain I've said that before.'

'Yes.'

'You've got those plastic pre-cut plasters. Not the stiff kind you have to cut yourself.'

'How do you know that?'

'When Coco came she had that kind of plaster on.'

'You say that like she was delivered to you every week wounded.'

'I asked her whether she'd put those plasters on her arm.'

'Miriam?'

'She was seven at the time. I explained to her that those are ugly plasters and that you should cut plasters from a big folded roll and they should feel stiff and dry. She'd forgotten. Even then.'

'Sorry.'

'It's a shame you've only come now. I have to sleep in the afternoons.'

'You can sleep. I'm just here.'

'When I wake up, you'll be gone. I'm not going to sleep.'

'I promise I won't be gone when you wake up.'

She closes her eyes and sniffs. She tries to smell him. He's too far away.

Wilbert is the tight plaster around her finger, the smell of pencils, dispelled later by the smell of beer. Wilbert is the taste of blood when he kisses her with his damaged lips after falling off his moped again. He is one of those cotton rucksacks with leather piping, which they all had at the time, in different colours. His was black and always a bit too heavy because he carried bottles of beer in it, in amongst the schoolbooks. You heard them clink against each other and Elisabeth is still amazed how few of them broke.

The rare bottle that broke in her bedroom replaced the pencil smell permanently with that of beer. It was a long Sunday afternoon, her parents had fallen asleep in the sitting room. The rays of sun made everything dustier, not more beautiful. You could taste the dust on Sundays. Your palate became rough, you wanted to eat all the time and then stop eating. Anything to get rid of the taste. Her sisters had left home already. The big attic bedroom was hers. She was like a pet that didn't require any attention, a cat that really just lives outside. You feed it and it goes its own way. She liked being that kind of animal. Wilbert had long stopped going into the sitting room when he came over, he just walked straight on up the stairs. She recognised the way he walked, he always skipped some stairs.

Wilbert didn't have a bottle opener. He always had bottles in that rucksack but never a bottle opener—as though he never intended to buy beer but hit upon the idea each day anew. He usually opened his bottles with a lighter. That Sunday he didn't have a lighter and tried to use the sharp edge of the radiator to whack the top off. The bottle broke. Foam and brown shards of glass on the carpet of her childhood bedroom. It was one of the few times that Elisabeth didn't consider the damaging of things a sign of decline. It was as though her bedroom had been inaugurated, as though it had merged with Wilbert. Now her whole bedroom smelled of him, and her bedroom smelled of him again every time the heating went on during the days that followed.

He sat on the floor with his back to the radiator and drank, faster than ever, at a speed he'd keep up for years. That was the moment he hit the right rhythm.

She opens her eyes. He is slumped backwards on the sofa holding a newspaper he must have brought with him. She doesn't get a paper.

He never drank faster than he had done in those days, but never slower either. Well, not until he stopped completely. But that doesn't say anything about the speed at which he'd drink if he allowed himself to.

The longer he sat in her bedroom drinking, the more often he said that she was beautiful, but he also asked, repeatedly, 'What do you want with someone like me?'

When he'd drunk enough, she'd dare answer, 'You are my dog, come and lie with me.' He looked at her with drunken eyes. He wanted to lie with her.

'Come,' she said. He crawled onto her bed and laid his head on her lap. She stroked him. 'You are my dog,' she said.

'My dog,' she said quietly, 'my dog.' He looks up from his paper.

'Do you want anything?'

'Come and lie with me.'

'Elisabeth...'

'Did I say something strange?' she asks, feeling amazed that she doesn't ask this question much more often, while god-knows-how-often she thinks it. He smiles. He doesn't want to answer. Ask again then. But it's the previous question she asks again.

'Come and lie with me?'

'Are those morphine plasters working a bit now?'

'Don't you ever drink anymore?'

'Not a drop.'

'I never minded when you were drunk.'

'I did.'

'I love you.' He doesn't speak. It doesn't matter. It's nice that she can say it. 'I love you so much.' He doesn't speak. 'Do you mind me saying that?'

'You don't love me, you love an idea.'

She searches for a superlative form of loving someone, of loving with heart and soul, but all she comes up with is his name.

'Wilbert.'

'You love a memory.'

'So you and Miriam love each other better?' She doesn't understand and will never understand it, she only understands that she failed and that her love doesn't count.

'Come and lie with me for a moment?' He kneels at her bedside and rests his head on the edge of the mattress. She smells the pencil shavings. She rests a hand on his head. She strokes him. She doesn't say: You are my dog. She doesn't say it out loud. She was always happy with her dog, but one day he didn't want to be her dog anymore. Miriam told him he had so many other names, and then he wanted them all. Names she didn't want to give him, she wanted her dog.

'I can be so much more,' he once said. 'And you can too,' he added afterwards. She could be so much more too. But who on earth wants that? To be more?

When the front door opens Wilbert scrambles to his feet. It's Coco and Miriam.

She looks at the broad-hipped woman and counts the times she's seen her in her life. How many birthdays?

Very quietly, Coco asks her father whether everything has gone well. Miriam nods amicably. Again Elisabeth thinks about vampires. Miriam was invited in just the once and now she's here again, as though that single invitation was sufficient for her to just walk in whenever she wanted from then on. For years Miriam has just been a name to her. Seldom has anyone taken so long to materialise.

'In the beginning I thought sometimes you might not exist at all.'

Miriam looks behind her, as though she's not the one being spoken to.

'You exist,' she says. No one speaks. 'A joke, I was making a joke... I think... Wasn't I?' Every bit of language she sends into the world has to be translated, explained, clarified. In her own bloody home.

When the doorbell rings, she remembers that the doctor was coming to visit and is suddenly delighted by all the people in her home. Especially now. *Are you telling people?* He will be pleased.

HER MOTHER SITS up in bed. Her cheeks seem to have some colour. Coco sits in between her father and stepmother, on the sofa at right angles to the bed. They sit in a ridiculous row facing the doctor, while he does his best to mainly address her mother.

Just before Peter Voors introduced himself as 'Peter Voors, GP,' Coco thought the tall man on the doorstep had come to sell them something. Miriam, of course, had been the first to say she'd leave them alone together, but her mother had gone to quite a lot of trouble to keep Miriam in the sitting room.

'Sit down, sit down, Miriam, sit down.' And Miriam sat down.

'Whatever you're comfortable with,' she said, but Coco thought: even if my mother was comfortable with you beating her with a chair, you shouldn't be comfortable with it. You shouldn't want to be here, but she saw that Miriam was all too eager to be here.

'How are you doing?' the doctor asks.

'Good,' her mother says, coughing. 'Sorry, good.'

She gives the doctor a friendly smile. Her father coughs now too. Miriam stares straight ahead, her mouth clamped shut, acting as though she knows her place and Coco just thinks: don't meddle, know my place, fucking hell, already asked too many bloody stupid questions. Know my place. I don't want to be the daughter, Coco thinks, the insatiable one with all the impertinent questions. When she was about fourteen things had got really complicated. On Tuesdays you still had the stepmother with her *You can tell me anything* to the point of tedium, and the next day there was the real mother who found the slightest question too much, too difficult, and on Thursdays the other one again, with her *How are you feeling, darling? How are you feeling?* Her father played along nicely. What Coco herself wanted to ask, wanted to know, wanted to say, disappeared into a very thick mist.

The doctor says, 'Listen, if the neighbours ask how you're doing and you don't feel like talking, you can just say "good," but when I ask how you're doing you can give me an honest answer.'

Her mother glances at Coco, as though asking for help.

'Because of course it isn't going that well,' the doctor says.

'No,' her mother says meekly, 'not so well, of course.'

Coco, her father, and Miriam, all three of them, look at the floor now. Three toddlers on a bench, thinks Coco. She's the boss of us all.

'How's it going with those pills I gave you?'

'Yes, I'm cutting down on them a bit,' her mother says, she looks proud, but Coco sees the doctor's concerned look.

'You mustn't do that. They reduce the pressure in your head. Will you please not do that? Why did you reduce the dose?'

'... I just wanted to. I just wanted to do it. Is that wrong?'

'You know you've got metastases in your head. You know that, don't you?'

'Yes, of course,' her mother says, 'I do know that.'

Coco's father looks at Coco and asks, almost silently, 'Did you know that?' Coco shrugs, and shakes her head angrily, like a teenager who thinks her father has asked a stupid question or at least at a stupid moment.

'Would you just take the prescribed dose of it?' the doctor asks.

'Oh, that's fine, no worries, if you think that's better,' her mother says in a tone that suggests she doesn't mind doing things for others.

'Mrs. De Wit,' the doctor says, 'you do understand the situation, don't you?'

And then Coco stands up, takes Miriam by the hand and pulls her from the sofa. 'We'll make coffee,' she says, and doesn't let go of Miriam's hand until she's on her way to the kitchen.

Just before she closes the kitchen door behind her, they just catch her mother giving the right answer. That she knows that it won't be long, that she's dying. Soon, yes. No, no, not months. Weeks. Perhaps not even that.

'I could die tomorrow,' she says. 'I do know,' proving to the doctor that she's not crazy, but extremely friendly.

'Bloody hell,' Coco says, 'that man is so serious.'

'The situation is serious,' Miriam says.

'Don't worry,' Coco says, 'the funeral's all taken care of.'

ELISABETH KEEPS DROPPING off to sleep and then waking up with a jolt from the same dream each time: that she's fallen asleep in the shop when she should be working, the frame has to be finished this afternoon. She gropes around for her tools, but the sound of glass wakes her up in the wrong space.

'Martin?'

It's Wilbert. He is sitting on the sofa, he bends down and picks up a glass. It isn't broken. He says, 'There wasn't anything in it.'

'What are you doing here?'

'You're not at work, Elisabeth, you're at home.'

'I know that, what are you doing here?'

'Coco made a roster—you remember, don't you?'

'Again?'

'It's still the same roster.'

'But you're here again.'

'Does that bother you?'

'I like it.' She is too tired to be polite. Too tired to think about what she should or shouldn't say. Again she sinks away, when she wakes up again the space is the right one. She sees what she expects to see and whom she expects to see.

'Hey,' she says.

'Hey,' he says.

'My dog.'

He doesn't speak.

'You are my dog.'

'I don't want to be a dog.'

...

'I don't want to be a dog.'

'I hear you.'

'Oh.'

'Did she let you come?'

'I'm my own man.'

Elisabeth smiles.

'Why are you smiling?'

'Did she say that? Did she say: "You're your own man"? Did she say that?'

'It's true, isn't it?'

'You're a dog who doesn't want to be a dog.'

'I'm not a... goddammit.'

'You don't want to be a dog, I know.'

Coco comes downstairs. They hear her go into the kitchen. The stairs are steep. Now that Elisabeth no longer goes up and down them herself, they are in her thoughts more than ever, due to that constant daughter-clatter. Coco has never gone up and down the stairs quietly.

'Does Coco have to go out?'

'I said I'd take over for this evening. Then she can pop out.'

Coco comes in. Elisabeth closes her eyes.

'Dad, are you sure?' Coco says it softly, she must think she's asleep. 'I don't really have to go out, you know.'

'But then you can pop round to Hans's.'

'Yes.'

'It's not a problem.'

'Does Miriam really not mind?'

'Jesus, I decide for myself, right?'

'But of course—it's Wednesday.'

'What's on Wednesdays?' Elisabeth asks.

'Did I wake you up?'

'What's on Wednesdays?'

'Miriam has yoga on Wednesdays,' Wilbert says, 'but that's not the point. What kind of a person do you take Miriam for? It was her idea.'

'Dog,' Elisabeth mumbles. He hears it. Coco doesn't, she's already walking away.

'I'm not the same man I was twenty years ago.'

'You're fatter.'

'That too, yes.'

'I'm not.'

'No.'

Coco stomps back upstairs.

When her daughter was two, she'd carry her down the steep stairs. One arm under those still-skinny buttocks. The child allowed this, step by step. And yet halfway down the stairs, she'd sense Coco preparing herself to fall. As soon as they had reached the bottom, she'd arch her back and slip out of her arms like a fish. Elisabeth tried to move with her—she didn't like to drop things— she wanted to be in control of how the things she was carrying were set down, how quickly they were released, but she'd just follow the fish as it fell. It wasn't uncommon for them both to be lying on the floor at the bottom of the stairs. The child would get up more quickly than she did, and Elisabeth would watch her go like someone who'd lost a contest. It wasn't yet seven o'clock in the morning, sometimes first light, usually still dark.

Before Elisabeth had got to her feet, the fish would have already become a different animal: a wild bull you've just freed and are watching carefully, hoping the fences will hold. Her daughter was many animals, but never a dog like her father, who used to let himself be stroked. Elisabeth would get up and as Coco ran to the heater, she had to rush and put herself between the two things.

'Whoa,' she'd say, 'whoa,' making herself broad, her arms spread. Wilbert was already at work then, and she'd look at the heater as though he was the heater, and think about the way he would sigh and say that it was nice for them to come downstairs to a warm room. It was years before she dared to say that it wasn't nice, before she understood that Wilbert wasn't the heater.

'I'd rather you turned the heater off before you left,' she said, but she said it too late and after too many of his questions.

Whether the warmth was nice, whether it was a nice thought, whether she realised...

'You said it was nice for us. I believed you.'

'I don't get you.'

'The-heater's-on. How-nice-that-must-be. That was what the heater was like.'

'But you didn't think it was nice?'

'It was nice... that it was supposed to be nice.'

'You're lying.'

'You're angry.'

'Why didn't you say so?'

'It was nice to see the heater and think: he does that for us.'

'But not anymore?'

'Yes, it is.'

'Should I leave it on or not?'

And so they destroyed their heater, which could no longer be on in the mornings and could no longer be off. The longer they talked to each other, the more Wilbert said that it was good that they were talking properly at last, and the bigger the areas of rot in the home became. Bit by bit everything became corroded, demolished, broken apart.

The largest injury, of course, was the sunroom window

that their girl had broken during her great flight to the outdoors. It ushered in the demolition. It was as though Coco knew better than her parents that it didn't really matter, because the decision to demolish had long been made.

'Should I get something out of the freezer?' Coco asks. 'Soup? Bread?'

'I'll have a look in a minute,' Wilbert says.

'You know where everything is.'

'Nothing's changed,' Elisabeth says. 'Everything's still in the same place.'

Again Coco walks away and returns. She is wearing her coat, a coat that is not made out of plastic and not made out of cloth. The coat makes a constant rustling, as though Coco is walking around in a giant newspaper. Doesn't she hear it herself?

'Do you still need me?'

Elisabeth and Wilbert sigh at the same time.

'Go,' her father says.

WHEN SHE RINGS the bell, he comes out of his practice, which is in the basement of his house.

He says, 'Laura's still here, we're preparing for Seattle.'

Coco waits for him to let her in and introduce her, but he unlocks the upstairs door and says, 'I'll be along in a minute.'

She didn't call him until she'd left her mother's house.

'Mum's deteriorating fast,' she said, 'Dad's with her, can I please come to yours for dinner? I have to get out for a bit.'

'Poor thing,' he said, 'it's getting too much, isn't it?'

'No,' she said, 'I just need to get out for a while, it's not too much for me! Christ!'

'... Would you please not shout at me.'

She cried because he seemed offended, because he was angry with her, and she could only think of one way to repair things quickly. So she just said: 'Sorry, yes, you're right. It is getting too much for me.' Crying made it believable.

She slowly mounts the steps to his house.

She sits down at the table, next to the newspaper. There's an empty wine glass next to the paper, an ugly green goblet. It's an heirloom and Hans often emphasises how precious the glass is to him and how she has to be careful with it. She deliberately shoves it aside roughly, because his warnings annoy her all of a sudden, he makes such a fuss, a thing like that doesn't break that easily, but mainly she doesn't just want to accept his warnings. The glass falls. She jumps, the goblet rolls still intact across the table in the opposite direction, see, things like that don't break that easily. But she jumps to her feet too quickly to grab it, bumps against the table, the glass rolls further and falls onto the floor. It breaks.

Sweat breaks out all over her body. Her hands tremble. She shakes her head.

Save me, she thinks, save me, and she knows that there is only one person who can.

She knocks on the window of the practice.

He doesn't open the door fully.

'Half hour, I'll be there.'

'I broke a glass.'

'Yes?'

'It's awful—it's the precious glass.'

'The green one?'

'Yes.'

'Yes,' he says, 'that is awful.'

'I wasn't careful, even though I was thinking...'

'Yes.'

'Of course, I knew that...'

'Let's not talk about it,' he says, 'it only hurts.'

'I'm sorry. I know it's important to you. I...'

'I mean it. I choose not to think about it then. It only hurts.'

'Sorry. It was...'

'Coco, stop. It's my glass. I don't want to talk about it. I'll be there in half an hour. OK?' He closes the door.

Breathing is difficult. The fear has not gone. Yet he won't mention it again. The glass no longer exists now.

Coco walks very carefully back up the steps, as though she'd never been downstairs. He mustn't hear her footsteps.

Coco wraps the broken glass in newspaper and puts it in her handbag, so that Hans doesn't have to see it again.

She is braced behind the newspaper when Hans comes in. She mustn't mention it. That would be egotistical, it's his glass, he can choose whether it existed or not, whether it broke or not.

'Are you done?'

'Yes.'

'Shall I make tea?'

'I've already had tea.'

'Something else?'

'I'll have a glass of wine. You won't, I guess?'

The word 'wine' makes her cringe internally. She feels dreadful and doesn't know if it's only to do with the glass. She thinks about that woman too.

'Is she pretty,' she asks, 'Laura?'

'Oh, Coco, please.'

That's not a good answer, but the question was worse.

'I'll reheat the Chinese from yesterday,' Hans says.

She accompanies him to the kitchen and sees the two trays he gets out of the fridge and thinks: no way is that enough.

'I'll have a drink with you,' she says. It's the final option. She doesn't see any other way out.

She wants to feel what she used to feel when she first got to know him. She wants him to feel that. It can't be gone. Sleep can't be all there is left. How pretty can Laura be?

They eat and they drink. After two glasses of wine she manages to ask him about his ambitions and not find it odd that someone wants something. After three glasses of wine she is able to take his counter-question seriously.

After four glasses of wine she can say that she doesn't want anything and that it is a big problem indeed. By the second bottle of wine, she says that she admires him and she doesn't know whether that's true.

She says, 'You... you are... the one for me. I've seen you. I've chosen you.'

'The way you chose which degree to take? The way you chose to move in with your mother?'

'I love my mother.'

'You can't just decide to love someone.'

'Shut up, man.'

'Talk to her.'

'You don't know what you're saying. Should you want to know *everything*? She is my mother. I am her daughter.'

'And I'm the one for you?'

'Yes, goddammit.'

'It's not going well, Coco, you can't deny that.'

'But you're going to see this through in the appropriate manner?'

'What's my keynote speech about?'

She empties the last glass, walks over to him and says, 'Overpower me.'

She sees it bothers him, but she also sees his pupils widen, and he kisses her. No, he eats. He devours. There's no difference between mouth, nose, cheek, ear, he devours her. And she doesn't just think: overpower me, she thinks: more, further. She thinks what she mustn't think. Hit me, beat me for god's sake, beat me senseless. The drink really gets the thinking going, she'd forgotten that. It makes the only interesting thoughts surface, the ones that are unreasonable but clear. She is so bad at thinking rationally, that's why she always comes across as sluggish and stupid, because she doesn't know the right arguments for the sensible thoughts. But she knows that she can hold forth for a long time on beat-me-senseless, which she hardly dares to think, she feels it, and one day there will be someone she'll dare say it out loud to. In the meantime he continues to devour her, you can't really call it kissing. He consumes her and she thinks about that girl—was it in England?—who wanted to commit suicide and took so many pills she didn't realise that her dog was eating her face. This is how he is chewing her and all she has to do is allow herself to be devoured, bite him back as quickly as possible, keep up with him, don't eat less than him. She pulls off his jumper, he hers, then vest, bra, and she cries and laughs and pants and eats and says without making a sound: Eating is the very, very, very best and most important of all things. She sucks his bottom lip. She wants to taste more than this and bites.

'Aah,' he says and she wants more of that sound too. She tastes blood, she sucks it up, together with his moans and again he says, 'Aah,' and pushes her off him.

'Jesus, you're biting me.'

For a moment Coco is stumped. Of course she is biting, you can't eat otherwise.

'What is this?' Hans asks and Coco doesn't answer: Eating. She has to stay calm. Act reasonable. This is not unusual. It went wrong with her first boyfriends. They always stopped. Everyone is afraid of all that emotion, and she is only afraid of not feeling anything anymore.

'Sorry,' she says, and, 'Oh no, you're bleeding,' as though she hadn't tasted his blood, swallowed it. She licks her own lips clean.

'Oh, my poor darling.' She kisses him gently. Gently on his cheek. Gently on his neck. Gently on his chest. His belly. She kneels. She hears his breathing quicken. She pulls his trousers down with great care. She pulls down his underpants with one hand, the other hand already nursing his cock. Don't frighten him. She restrains herself and she cries because when it comes down to it, when she is awake, finally awake, when the alcohol has kissed her awake, she is always quicker than the other. She licks his cock and he groans and closes his eyes and hasn't seen through her tears. She takes all of him in her mouth, shields her teeth, expands her lips and bites and slides and sucks and tastes snot and spit and tears and somewhere in the distance, blood.

She stops and takes a deep breath.

'Come with me,' he says, pulling her up and pushing her towards the bedroom. He pulls off her trousers and pushes her onto the bed, a little wildly, thank god. She falls. He moves over her, too big and too heavy and she mustn't say: Crush me, pulverise me, murder me, for god's sake kill me, do something that feels worse than this. He pushes a leg aside, enters her, cock in her, his limbs against hers, and thrusts and glides and thrusts, pulls back and thrusts into places she can't reach. And that is the secret of everything, places she can't reach. It all needs to be faster and deeper and worse, but then there is his final thrust already, he shudders and as his sweaty body drops onto her she starts crying where she left off, because she knows it isn't enough. She crawls out from under him, he rolls onto his side and falls asleep. How is it possible that this gives satisfaction, peace, to another? A big baby lies next to her. Coco is wide awake. It is not enough. She wipes her tears. It doesn't matter. She just has to go and get more. She can do that.

She gets up and puts her clothes on. When she's drunk, she's five. She thinks about leaves when she's drunk, and then she wants to go outside, walk through them, like it was always autumn when she was five. There must have been an autumn when she could do anything. She remembers how certain she was of everything, knowing that she could jump over a much too big puddle, and how certain she was the others would listen to her if she told them what to do.

Once she told the boy next door who was the same age as her that it was possible to jump out of the bedroom window.

'You just have to bend your knees a lot when you land, that's very important. I've done it a lot of times. You really can.' She talked him into it, until he climbed onto the windowsill and went to open the window. Only then did she say that it had been a joke. But it was pleasurable being able to get another person to go this far.

She looks at the sleeping man and is sure she has the upper hand. Whoever is awake has the upper hand. She won't sleep anymore. She is sure she doesn't need sleep now.

Hans doesn't hear a thing. Hans doesn't believe in it. Poor Hans, he doesn't see it. It'll come.

She stops on the pavement outside his house. Her handbag won't close because it's got the newspaper with the broken glass in it. She pinches at the paper but doesn't cut herself. She crosses the street without paying any attention to the traffic and that goes well.

'I'm back,' she says as she walks into the centre. The city centre is her friend.

She goes into the first pub she sees, an Irish pub. She pauses and looks around and thinks: you can have me, before looking for a seat, taking off her coat. It doesn't take long for men to look at her. It is even easier than it used to be. She has forgotten why she didn't want this anymore. Why did she give this up? This is so much better than eating. Better than sleeping too. Now things will come right. Now she has this again, she can stop sleeping, eating, Hans, everything.

There is a football match on a screen in one corner. That's good, directs the gaze. She walks past the screen, takes off her coat, orders beer, leans against the bar, and watches Ireland play Estonia.

'If you sit here,' a man taps her on the shoulder, pointing at a stool next to him, 'you'll have a better view.'

Her eyes slide over his body, his face. Possible. Now all he has to do is not say anything too stupid.

Whether she likes football? What she thinks of the Irish pub? If she wants another beer? If she's cold? No? She seems to be trembling. Oh, she isn't. Just a shiver?

It almost goes wrong when he says, 'I think you must be very sensitive.'

She laughs loudly, 'No, that I'm not.'

He laughs too, that makes a difference, that helps, now don't say anything else like that. Shut him up.

'You've got a bit of blood on your cheek.'

'Yes,' he says, 'cut myself shaving.'

She reaches towards it, touches the small wound. Obvious, she has touched him, the rest is up to him now.

'It's all right, it's not bleeding anymore,' she says. As she goes to the toilet, she sees that he's afraid it's an excuse. He is tall. When she returns, she stays standing on the ledge that runs along in front of the bar so that she can look him in the face more easily, he takes a step closer. He kisses her and it feels good. Full, soft. Then he hugs her. It is very strange, his face moved past hers all of a sudden and now it's resting on her shoulder. She breaks free.

'No cuddling?' he asks, and the word disturbs her for a moment, it's such a strange word for in a pub. She lays a finger across his lips.

'Sshh.' She kisses him and then his hands knead her waist. Good, his hands are hungry, then it's all right, then it's possible. Although she could just go home now, because she knows it won't be enough.

Coco stands in the middle of the sitting room and smiles at her mother. Her father left as soon as she got home.

'Are you drunk?' her mother asks.

'Yes.'

'Oh, my darling,' she says, 'did you have a nice time?'

'Yes. Quite.'

'I wish I liked it. Always said that to your father. But I don't like the taste.'

Coco nods and stumbles.

'Poor child.'

'Sorry,' Coco says, she's kneeling.

'Have you hurt yourself?'

'I nodded a bit too hard.'

'Do you want anything else?'

'What have you got then?'

'Not much, just a bottle of port—for Martin, but he never drinks much.'

Coco is still kneeling and asks, 'Have you never wanted another relationship?'

Her mother appears to reflect.

'Or am I not speaking clearly?' Coco asks.

'No, I can understand you.'

'Have you never wanted another husband?'

'Yes,' her mother says, 'but which one?'

Coco thinks about the man from the Irish pub. She wants him again but knows that a different man would be better, before he too turns into someone in whose arms she wants to gently fall asleep. It's too late for Mum, but not for me.

'I commit too easily,' she says, drunk enough to forget who she's talking to.

'I've got that too,' her mother says.

'I latch onto a man right away.'

'You always had boyfriends,' her mother says, 'right from secondary school.'

'I always latch on. I like to latch on. But then I die slowly, do you know what I mean?'

'I'm not sure.'

'Then the water stops moving, right? Then it gets stagnant.'

'A fish has to swim.'

'Yes, know what I mean?'

'Yes.'

'And now the floodgates have broken.'

'Are you the water or the fish?'

Coco ponders this. 'I'm a fish,' she says, 'but I want to be the water.'

Her mother closes her eyes.

'Are you tired?'

'Very tired.'

Coco turns off the lights in the sitting room and wishes her mother goodnight.

'I'll be quiet on the stairs,' she says, and she slips out of the house again. There's a bar on the street corner. It's not even that it has to happen again right away, she just has to check whether it can happen again, whether it works. After that some sleep will be all right.

COCO HAS RUN around the house all day. Up the stairs, down the stairs. She has fetched glasses of water. If Elisabeth didn't drink them, Coco would change the water. She made sure that the telephone was within arm's reach. Set the base under it, crawling under the bed to find the socket.

'There, now the battery can't go flat. I think of everything.'

She made bouillon, kept making fresh coffee, drank it herself. She ran to the off-licence to buy port for Martin, but called three times on the way.

What's going on with the roster, who's replacing the child?

She has hardly moved today, but she has heard much too much movement.

'You're incapable of empathising,' Wilbert used to say. A lie. When Coco runs, she runs too. When Coco screams, she screams too. When Coco eats, she chews just as fast. By the end of the day she is shattered.

Now when the doorbell rings and she waits for the wild child to escape through the door and the peace to return, the room is full of people all of a sudden: Wilbert, Coco, and Miriam.

'Are you in the roster too?' she asks Miriam.

'It's Martin's turn, we're just popping in,' Wilbert says, 'Miriam wanted to drop round.' He can't cope with her. Yesterday evening he'd become more and more silent and when Coco got home he'd practically run out of the house.

'Can I do anything?' Miriam asks. Nobody replies.

Wilbert says, 'I'm going to bleed the radiators, I don't think it's been done for years,' and leaves the room.

'He's having a hard time of it,' Miriam says.

'It really is necessary actually,' Coco says, 'the radiators make a horrible racket,' and she's off again.

Miriam comes closer. 'He finds it really difficult, he doesn't say so, but I can tell.' She sits down on the sofa next to the bed.

Elisabeth can't take any more. She pants. She doesn't want to feel sympathy for this woman. She wants to forget her.

She says, 'Yes, I know, he loves me,' she is almost out of breath, 'he can't look at me without loving me. That's why he doesn't look at me.'

Miriam's face becomes more ugly than it already was. It's because of the pity. Elisabeth gives Miriam a painful smile and waits. Then the pity disappears from Miriam's face on its own. She gets it. Miriam gets it now—the fact that she's right.

'Of course... you have a place... in his heart.'

'He's a dog,' Elisabeth says, 'would you fetch me a glass of water?'

'He's not a dog.'

'Yes, he likes that, you saying he's not a dog, but we both know he is a dog. Would you fetch me some water?' She sinks away. Everything goes black.

She starts when she suddenly sees Coco, standing in front of her in that crackling coat.

'I'm off.'

There's that girl again, the one who always fell out of her arms. The smile is back and she seems much thinner now. Faster. Like she used to be. She realises that you can't hold onto that body—it will just slide away again. She feels that her arms are useless and cries.

'Are you in pain?' Wilbert asks, standing on the doorstep with a bucket in his hand and a towel over his shoulder.

'My arms,' she says, 'my arms aren't made for that, for holding a fish. I can't do anything about it.'

'Of course you can't do anything about it,' Wilbert says, slowly coming closer.

'Fish?' Miriam asks.

'My arms,' she says, because her arms are leaden and weak.

'Fish?'

'The fish is off,' Coco says.

'No!' Miriam screams, standing up. 'Coco is not a fish!'

Elisabeth smiles. Coco does too. Wilbert glances quickly from Coco to Elisabeth—his eyes as light as back then—before going over to Miriam. For a brief moment, just before he went over to her, they were a family. So that's how it feels. She would have been better off with an enemy.

'SOMETHING… THAT I'm… genuinely… interested in?'
Coco slowly repeats his question and tries to win time.
She is in Hans's kitchen and squeezes a silver-coloured
plastic bag containing cheese fondue into a pan. She had
called him and said, 'I want to talk.' She couldn't think of
a better reason to invite herself over, a reason that would
be sufficient for him, this was the last one left.

She thinks about the previous evening and the second pub she visited. There was a short man with very
thin lips who kissed amazingly gently. She thinks about
his hand on her buttocks, still in the pub, it kept ventur-
ing downwards. Fingering in an alleyway. All she could
think with each new step was: aha, yes, that's all right.
Now this then. Yes, that's all right too. Is he going to
kneel? Yes, he's going to kneel, I see it. She'd recorded the
experience like an accountant. Too drunk to make more
of it than that: keep a tally, record, name, know, and who
knows: remember and that's how it comes back now, like
a list: hand, fingers, tongue.

'Something that I'm… genuinely interested in, Yes, we
were talking about that yesterday.' Yes, she's interested
in that, in the things the accountant keeps track of.

'It's good that we're talking,' he says.

'Why? You don't believe in us.'

'I like to understand things.'

'I went to the Irish pub.'

'When? Yesterday?'

'Yes.'

'Alone?'

'Yes… I kissed a stranger.' She doesn't look at him. The

cheese fondue is lying in a large rectangular slab in the pan.

'Oh sweetie, even kissing's quite a thing for you.'

'You're not jealous?'

'Not if it doesn't mean anything.'

'It doesn't... mean anything... Not in the way you meant.'

'I'd prefer not to know that kind of thing.'

'It wasn't all that happened...'

'I don't need to know this.'

She hacks at the slab of cheese with a wooden spoon and stirs the chunks in the increasingly hot pan. She is so keen to tell him about a strange man licking her out in the alleyway next to the good chippie, but she waits until he says, 'Or it has to be very important for you.' She misses the girl she was friends with in the local pub last year. She could have got through it with her, they would have sat there exactly like this. There would have been somebody in the middle to tell it all to.

'It's good that we're talking.'

'Yes,' she says, waiting for instructions, waiting for the conversation leader to tell her what she should talk about.

'What you genuinely want now, that's what we were talking about. What are you really interested in?'

'Are you sleeping with Laura?'

'No.'

'Not yet.'

'I'm not sleeping with her.'

'But you love her.' There's silence. She says it again. 'You love her.'

'I could love her.'

'But you don't?'

'It would be possible to.'

'But...'

'I want to talk about you, about us, not about Laura.'

'Not about Laura, not about strange men, not about the broken glass.'

'Men? Plural?'

'We're not talking about that, Hans. Or it has to be important for you. Is it important to you?'

'Coco, what are you doing here?'

'I'm making a cheese fondue.'

'You think you love me.'

'That's all there is,' she says. 'Nothing has any flavour. Do you understand? I can say that this pre-packaged fondue tastes nice, but I can also say it's disgusting. If I think about it, I don't know.'

'So you'd rather not think about it?'

She looks at him and doesn't want to talk but drink. 'I don't know what I'm doing here.' The cheese fondue boils.

'You need to stir it.'

'Stir it yourself.'

'Coco, it's burning.'

'Stir it then.'

He grabs the wooden spoon from her and stirs.

'Bastard,' she says.

'Coco, please.'

She can't breathe. She wants to swear at him, she wants to hit him, she wants to hurt him and for him to love her. No, she wants to kill him and for someone to console her. No, she wants...

'I have to go,' she says.

'Does it have to be like this?'

'I really have to go,' she says. 'Sorry,' she says, as she puts on her coat, 'I really have to go, we'll talk later. I have to go. I can't do this.' She practically runs out of the house.

She takes a deep breath outside his door. Then she begins to walk. Fast, like a race-walker. She walks towards her mother's house. It's too far, but she doesn't want to get in a tram, doesn't want to sit, doesn't want to be warm.

Good, it's dark, but the supermarkets are still open and there are still too many people on the street on their way home from work. Too many raincoats, too many shopping bags. She has to find a bar where it's been dark all day, or where night begins at six.

Halfway between Hans's house and her mother's, she finds a pub with Shrovetide decorations and Christmas lights in the windows. The glass is sufficiently grimy.

The door jams and opens with a jerk. It is like walking into a stranger's living room, but the smell of beer and washing up liquid makes it immediately appealing, welcomes her in. A single barkeeper and just one man at the bar. Good. More isn't necessary. You have to keep an open mind.

She sits down at the bar opposite the man—it's a horseshoe shaped bar—and orders a beer. The men are talking about football. Coco looks at the man facing her. He isn't ugly. She guesses he's in his mid-forties. He's wearing a necklace with his name on it. John. His body is strong and good.

If she can make sure he doesn't talk, it'll be possible. Or if she can make sure she's so drunk his words become beautiful. It's a pity she doesn't like spirits, a pity she needs all that time and litres of beer to get her where she needs to be.

After the second beer, John says, 'Give the young lady a beer from me.'

She nods. Later holds up the pint. 'Thanks.'

It's all so pathetic and ugly, like plasticky slabs of fondue in silver bags. But in an hour that will all be over. Just a matter of sitting and drinking.

'What does it say?' she asks after she's bought him a pint in return. She points at his chain.

'My name,' John says.

'Can't read it from here,' Coco says and she gets up and walks up to him. 'John. Hi, John. John, like John Denver?'

'Just John,' John says. 'What's your name?'

'Tammy,' Coco says.

'Do you like John Denver?' John asks.

'Country roads, take me home,' Coco sings.

'To a place, I belong,' John sings.

'West Virginia, mountain mama. Dance with me,' Coco says, taking his hand and pulling him off his bar stool.

'Got any John Denver?' John asks the barman. The barman turns around slowly and looks at a small laptop. John and Coco shuffle round in a circle, his hands resting cautiously on her hips, her arms around his neck, her face close to his ear. He smells of shampoo and beer.

'Almost heaven, West Virginia,' Coco whispers.

'Blue Ridge Mountain, shining dough a river,' John sings.

'What did you just sing?' Coco asks.

'What?'

'Blue Ridge Mountain, and then?'

'Shining dough a river.' He takes her hand and tries to spin her around. Coco breaks free.

'No, John, it's *Shenandoah* River, That's a river, that's what it's called. Shenandoah River. Do you know what you were singing? You were singing: shining dough a river. Like magic bread dough and a river.'

Everything is ruined. Bloody hell, a man who sings

John Denver lyrics phonetically. She feels almost sober.

'Anal bitch.' He says it quietly but aggressively.

She feels it immediately in her stomach and the alcohol again in her head. Well done, John. John is evil. John is dangerous. That's nice. Now John can say as many stupid things as he wants.

'You might not be clever,' Coco says, 'but perhaps you're really good at other things.'

'Maybe we'll have to teach you a lesson,' John says.

'I want to learn,' Coco says, 'I really want to learn, I'm a student.'

'Give the lady something stronger,' John says to the barman.

'I don't like spirits.'

'You have to *learn* to drink them,' John says, 'you want to learn, don't you?'

That's true, she wants to learn. He gives her jenever and it's not long before her head is large and heavy and she complains about it and lays it on his shoulder.

'I told you so, didn't I.'

'You don't need your head,' John says, 'what's your name again?'

'I'm Tammy and I always stand by my man.'

'Your man? Are you married?'

She lifts her heavy head from his shoulder. 'No, John, I'm quoting.'

'You're an odd one, you know that?'

'I'm a beginner. I'm learning. You have to help me,' and then she knows what she wants to say and she says it too: 'I also want to know what it's like to fuck a stranger, right in the middle of a pub, when someone might come in at any moment. I want to learn that,' Coco says. John gets a crazed look. She sees it.

'You're messing with me, you're taking the mickey,' John says.

'I'm as pissed as a newt, man, you can do anything you want to me.'

John looks afraid now and she says, 'Don't tell me you're a good guy after all.'

'Hey,' John says, 'I might be a bit crude and I didn't go to university, Miss Tammy, but I am a good guy.'

'So you're not going to fuck me?'

'You should watch your mouth.'

She feels tears coming. 'Fucking hell, John. Hold me.'

'How old are you?' John asks. That age thing again. Now she feels calm. She has to be. Crying and begging never works.

'Shall I give you a blow job?' she asks in an even tone of voice. His eyes widen. More politely perhaps: 'Please may I give you a blow job?' She notices that the barman can hear everything and is practically frozen to the spot. John looks panicked now.

Then the barman says, 'You can give me a blow job.'

Coco studies the barman. He is a little older than John. A bit fatter too, and a bit balder.

'And how old are you?' Coco asks.

'Not going to start getting picky, are you?'

'No. I'll give you a blow job in here.'

'Here?'

'All right then,' Coco says, 'behind the bar.'

'We could pop out back.'

'No, only if I can do it behind the bar.'

John and the barman look at the door of the pub. Coco too.

'The door can't be locked,' Coco says. 'I'll only give you a blow job behind the bar if someone could walk in at any minute.'

The barman slowly nods and puts down the glass he's been polishing for much too long. Coco walks over to the bar and feels the exaltation inside and thinks: what a great story I'll have to tell after this. If there was anyone I could tell a story like that to.

She needs to concentrate to keep her heavy head upright as she sinks to her knees behind the bar. It has got so big and all kinds of unfortunate associations are coming to her. She thinks of the woman on Oprah Winfrey talking about a helicopter accident. The woman saw her husband who was horribly burned; he was alive but only just. His head had grown to twice the size and she wondered for a moment: Who is that man? the man with the strange big head, and then that head said: I love you, and she recognised him. I love you, Coco says to her own head now, but you have to stay upright for a bit longer on your thin neck, I need you.

She undoes his belt, a cheap plastic belt in a pair of brown corduroy trousers. The trousers are already hanging low under his large belly. The big trousers fall down unassisted. Using both hands she tugs the white underpants down over his bottom, takes hold of his cock.

'A pleasant cock you've got there,' she says. And now smells come to her, but it's as though she can only name them, not smell them. As though the words have merely been written down: gingerbread—nutmeg—dishcloth —mushrooms.

You can do it, she thinks as she takes the stranger's cock in her mouth and looks at the buckets behind the man, under the sink cabinet.

'Oh, oh, Tammy,' he says. And Coco thinks: I can do anything. Everything is possible. I can make everything possible. Wherever I am, everything is possible. She hears John laugh, a nervous giggle.

'You know,' he begins, 'it's not the size of the boat but the motion on the ocean.'

Coco stops sucking off the barman and says, '*Of*—the motion *of* the ocean.' And then the jenever rises up, with painful jerks and jolts, with horrific sounds that hardly match the precision with which she vomits so neatly into the bucket behind the barman.

'I told you so,' she says, 'I can't handle spirits.' She shakes. 'I'm ill,' she says, 'I want to go home.'

She stands up, wobbles over to her coat, grabs it, staggers out of the pub, and sinks back down onto her knees and vomits outside, just next to the door. She lies down for a while with her cheek on the rubber mat that consists of countless circles. A soft mat, she could stay here for a while. The supermarkets are probably closed now. It's quieter on the street. She gets up. She has to relieve Martin, she has to be home on time. It's nice to have to be home on time for someone. She looks at her telephone to see whether they have called her already, where she's got to. No messages.

'Yes, yes,' she says, 'I'm on my way, I'm on my way already.'

'You're early,' her mother says.

'I'm a bit ill.'

Martin gets up. Coco looks at the bottle of port on the stool next to her mother's bed. It's still almost full.

'Do I need to put you to bed too?' Martin asks.

'I can look after myself,' Coco says, 'you go.'

'Just a joke, Coco.'

'We don't have much of a sense of humour,' Coco says, 'do we, Mum?'

Martin ignores her. He kisses her mother's forehead. Coco stands next to him and watches, too ill to turn away her gaze. She lets her coat, which she hadn't put on but had dragged along behind her, drop to the floor.

Martin almost trips over it as he goes to leave.

'Child,' her mother says.

When he's gone, she lies down on the sofa.

'I had too much to drink.'

'Your father drank too much too, but I never minded.'

'Who are you?'

...

'I'm your mother.'

'Yeah, that's right, isn't it?'

'Yes.'

'Do you think I'd make a good mother?'

'Of course,' her mother says kindly.

Coco smiles. 'Thank you.'

'When you were lying next to me in bed, just after you'd been born, I thought: who is this?'

'And then?'

'It stayed, that's what's so nice about it. That it stays.'

'Nice.'

'Yes.'

'I've heard say,' Coco begins, 'that what women actually think is: oh, so you're it?'

'Oh yeah?'

'Yeah.'

'Never heard that.'

'No?'

'Can't be true.'

'So if you've never heard it, it can't be true?'

'They all think of themselves. They see themselves and recognise that. They only think of themselves, but they don't realise it—that they only think of themselves.'

'How many of those morphine plasters have you got on?'

'You'll have to ask Martin, he keeps a note of everything.'

'I can't undo these ties on my blouse.'

'Come here.'

Coco lets herself slide off the sofa and crawls to her mother. 'They're really fiddly.'

Her mother's hands shake.

'It's a Chinese blouse.'

'Yes, Chinese. I don't know if I can do it.'

'We're in no hurry.'

'One of them is open but that second one is tighter.'

'I gave a stranger a blow job in the pub.' Her mother continues to fiddle with the second tie. 'Behind the bar.'

'Do you have an open relationship? You and Hans?'

'Very open, yes.'

'Can't do it. Why do you wear such complicated clothes?'

'It's a nice blouse. Tell me it's a nice blouse, Mum.'

'It's a nice blouse.'

'Thank you, it's a Chinese blouse. I got it from Hans.'

'I've never been good at jealousy.'

'Good at jealousy?'

'Or always too late. A person has to be jealous. Right?'

'Has to be?'

'He held it against me. "You didn't know where I was," he said. I wasn't interested in where he was. I wasn't there, was I? How can something interest me when I'm not there? Should I open your belt for you too?'

'Can do it myself.'

'Belts are difficult. I always had to help your father with his belt. Drunk people always pull the buckle the wrong way.' Her mother loosens her belt. 'Just pull your blouse over your head. That knot is too tight. I'm shaking too much.'

'There are mothers and daughters who hug each other,' Coco says.

'Do you want that?'

'I don't think so.'

'If you don't want it,' her mother says, 'we won't do it.'

Coco stands up. 'You live in a fun neighbourhood, all those pubs.'

'Yes, it's a shame you don't go into them that much.'

'Hmm.' Coco takes two steps. 'I think I need to throw up.' She hurries to the kitchen, just making it to the sink in time.

When she wakes up, long before daybreak, and remembers the day before, there's no shame. On the contrary. The thought that she can do everything endures and she knows it's just as easy to carry on conversations with her mother this drunk. Nothing is stopping her now: no embarrassment, no fear, no love.

THERE SHE GOES again. She hears the parquet flooring creak. She opens her eyes briefly. It's not even light yet. It's that same thing again, it always happens. She's had it since the first day. Coco wasn't even an hour old. Elisabeth had taken a shower, sitting on a wooden stool with a plastic bag over it. The midwife had supported her as she walked back to her bed. She had only just laid down in it, turned her head and started. There was the child, she'd already forgotten about it. It wasn't a horrible shock to find the baby there, but it was a big surprise.

'Right, we need to have a little talk about it,' Coco says.

Elisabeth jumps again. 'What time is it then?' she asks.

Coco doesn't answer, she comes closer. She sits on the foot of the bed, her legs crossed. She pushes her legs.

'Shove up.'

Elisabeth gets up then and pulls her legs up towards her. 'It's still dark.'

'About the fall,' Coco says. 'We need to talk about the fall.'

Elisabeth understands what her daughter means straight away.

There's nothing about the fall that Coco doesn't know, but she seems to sense that there are conclusions, thoughts connected to it, which have never been expressed. And yet Elisabeth is not afraid of anything. She knows what to say. Eight years of practice, then you have your story down to a tee. She is tired. Sitting begins to weigh on her.

She closes her eyes and speaks like the voice-over in a

documentary: 'You had just turned five when you cycled through the sunroom window. You fell, keeping your hands on the handlebars.'

Coco says the last bit with her: '... keeping your hands on the handlebars.' For a moment, Elisabeth hopes that Coco likes the familiar construction and isn't looking for any new words—the way you keep reading a child the same story and they want you to stick to the text in the book. But when she opens her eyes, she sees that Coco doesn't want a story. She won't leave until they've recreated the memories together, until they have uncovered new meanings, as yet unused words, fresh combinations forming unexpected sentences. She closes her eyes and lets her daughter fall again, shards of glass behind her.

She was in the garden and had already heard her daughter's bicycle bell. The stabilisers had just been taken off. The bike was in the hall. Coco knew only too well she wasn't allowed to cycle in the house. Elisabeth was standing with her back to the house when she heard the glass breaking. It sounded like a bang, a shot. When she turned around, her daughter was there, in the air, between shards and bike—making real what Elisabeth feared. She had been right. Tick.

Elisabeth observed the scene and let Coco, the glass and the bike hang frozen in the air and took a deep breath and exhaled. After five years she breathed in and out again. So this is what it is, she thought. Here is where it ends. She has fallen at last. Her relief had nothing to do with happiness, but at the same time it did—she hadn't ever wanted to explain this to anyone.

She opens her eyes. She doesn't bother to avoid Coco's gaze. They look at each other, like two cats in a face-off.

'I saw you fall,' Elisabeth says.

'I know.'

'I mean, I saw you die.' Coco doesn't say anything. 'I've seen you die twice. Once in the air and once in room 14.'

When the child landed on the gravel paving stones, instead of the silence and settlement she expected, there was screaming and blood. Suddenly the beautiful moment in which shards and Coco hung so silently in the air was over. The peace, the exhalation, and the inevitable ending with all its unavoidable pain, lay on a path that she shouldn't have taken. A wrong turn. She had thought it was over, but it wasn't.

Coco becomes hazy. Elisabeth's vision is getting steadily worse. She knows her daughter is sitting close to her, but getting to her seems impossible. The foot of the bed is too far away.

She talks to the hazy child, 'I was sent to room 14. The door was open a chink. Wilbert had to be there somewhere. He had gone in the ambulance while I sorted things out at home. They never forgave me that. Clearing up the glass.'

'They?'

'I cut open some bin bags and taped them to the window frame with masking tape. I'd already called a glazier. He was called Herman. He was going to see whether he could come that same day.'

Elisabeth knows how she and Wilbert talked about it later—that she must have been in a real panic. She must have been so shocked that she concentrated on something manageable. They said: Some people shine in an emergency; other people's weaknesses come to the fore.

'I let Herman in, he came much earlier than expected.'

'Herman.'

'Herman Siezen. Like the newsreader. But then Herman rather than Harman.'

'That you still remember that.'

'I know. I was very clear-minded. Very calm.' She doesn't tell her about the sound the bin bags she'd taped to the window made. 'And then I got a tram to the hospital.'

'Why didn't you take a taxi?'

Elisabeth would like to stretch out her legs but Coco's in the way.

'Why didn't you take a taxi?'

'I must have been in deep shock.'

'You just said you were very clear-minded.'

'You remember the strangest things, yes.' Then she stretches out her legs carefully, a little, but feels Coco already, so pulls them back up again.

'You took a tram.'

'There was a direct line.'

'Why not a taxi? Why not faster? Didn't you want to be with me?'

'I must have been in deep shock.' Coco is silent. What more does she want? Ugly words then. 'Survival strategy,' she says. 'It must have been a survival strategy.' She no longer has a clue what she is saying when she adds more strangeness like: repression, inhibition, projection. She is just babbling. There is an infinite number of ugly words. If Coco wants them so much, she's going to get them. She looks at the blot at the foot of the bed. 'I was sent to room 14,' she says. It does seem as though a blot hears less than a clearly outlined daughter.

'That's where I was,' the blot says.

'No,' Elisabeth says, 'you weren't.'

'I was in room 14.'

'No. I looked inside and you weren't there. There was only an injured child. It was dark, the curtains were closed and that child was badly injured. I saw that, and it had its eyes closed.'

'Me?'

'Not at the time. Not yet. You weren't... a nurse was standing behind me and she... She didn't push me, but... she stood so close to me, as though she wanted to prevent me from going back, So I took a step forwards into the room on my own and then I turned around to the nurse and I said, "That's not her."

"Yes, it is," the nurse said again and took a step, so that I had to take another step, because otherwise she'd be standing too close to me. She chased me into that room.'

"'Just go inside," she said and so I did that, out of politeness really. But once I was there, it was you after all.'

Elisabeth remembers how her stomach had filled with stones, like the wolf in the fairy tale. She walked into the room with leaden steps and the injured child became her daughter. Just like that. Wham. No, bam. No. A slurping sound. Something that takes everything away, sucks it in, eats it up.

The image of her girl slid off that of the injured child and stayed there. She felt it falling into place. It fit so perfectly that right away you could no longer see that what you were looking at consisted of two images. The child opened her eyes. She was what they call weak.—How is she? Weak.—There were only a few spaces and only a few words fit into them. It was just light enough to be able to see each other. No light or sound was wasted here.

'Hello, little girl,' she said to her.

'Mummy,' the girls said. The first words were easy. Now wait calmly until she knew which ones should follow.

'Daddy was frightened,' she said.

'Is Daddy angry?'

'Daddy isn't angry.'

'And you?'

'You're my girl. You're going to sleep now,' and the girl smiled and closed her eyes. Walk away now. Elisabeth smiled too. Now it was over. That was how you said the last words.

But after the last words the girl just came back again.

'I thought you were dying,' Elisabeth says.

'I find it strange you should say that.' Coco sounds calm. Elisabeth knows that she hasn't lied, not about this.

'I swear, I thought you were dying.'

'I had a broken leg and some cuts, you don't die of that.'

'I thought it!'

'Why did you think it?'

'When you crashed through the window...'

'Yes, I understand that, that you might think that *then*. But why in the hospital?'

'Shards of glass in the neck can be very dangerous.'

'Come on, you already knew I wasn't bleeding to death, that's rubbish.'

'I don't understand. What do you want? I don't understand.'

'No, you do know, Mum, you know very well. I know about your memory. And still you act all vague.'

'I thought that, because... Because we were so...' It's impossible to tell the truth. That it was a lovely and acceptable ending and that she had reconciled herself to that ending. So she says, 'I must have been in deep shock.'

HER MOTHER IS just lying there now, her eyes closed all of the time. She doesn't say anything anymore. She doesn't sleep. Her mouth is tense.

'Mum?' Coco thinks about the wooden box full of blocks she had as a child. You had to put a triangle, a square, and a star into it, through holes with the same shape. You had to take the whole lid off to get them out again. It's too long ago but Coco still thinks she remembers not opening the lid but holding the box upside down and shaking it until the blocks fell out. It didn't work, however hard she shook it. She'd been shaking her mother that way for years and she still felt like she was the stupid one, someone who doesn't know that there's a much easier way: a loser, a baby. It got light. The paleness of her mother's arms and hands became less noticeable than in the darkness, but her thinness more so. Yet it is theoretically possible that if you keep on shaking, a block will fall out. If you could shake for infinity, if you were inexhaustible. Coco smiles.

'Mum?... Mum?' The doorbell rings. 'Hey, Mum.'

'The door,' her mother says.

'Mum,' she says, 'Mum, Mum, Mum,' as though Mum isn't a word but a sound, as though it mimics the shaking of the blocks.

'Mumumumumumumumumumumumum.'

'The door, Coco!'

'I'm relieving you,' says Martin.

She's standing at the door in her pyjamas.

When he's inside, he repeats, 'I'm relieving you. You're free.'

'Oh, yeah,' Coco says and goes upstairs to get dressed, comes back down and puts on her coat—as though Martin had given her an order: You're free, go.

Coco exits the street but doesn't know where she's going. Hans will be impressed that she provoked her mother like that.

He said once, 'It seems like you're afraid of her.' She wants him to see her, to see what she is capable of, what she dares to do. There's a bench next to the tram stop, she sits down on it.

'Speak Russian,' he'd said to her the first time they were out together. She spoke Russian.

'What did you just say?'

'I was quoting from that book.'

'What did you say then?'

'Her hair hangs in pretzel-shaped plaits over her ears, and she has ribbons and bows in her hair: black ribbons, or blue ones, or white, or brown; Fima has a lot of ribbons. Seryozha wouldn't even have noticed but Fima asked him herself, "Have you seen how many ribbons I have?"'

'That's why you decided to study Russian? To be able to translate that?'

She said, 'Have you seen how many ribbons I have?'

He looked a little bewildered, as though he hadn't yet decided whether he found this quite stupid or quite extraordinary.

When the tram that goes to her house arrives, she gets in. Her mother's words, which she has known for so long, reverberate around her head: *Must have been in deep shock. Must have been in deep shock.*

I'm going back to university, Coco decides. I've been asleep for part of this year, but now I've woken up.

When she gets out, she sees him sitting in the Coffee Company, opposite the tram stop, at a table in front of the window with a woman who must be Laura. She knows they meet there a lot—in the morning before the first consultation. There's a lot to do for a conference like that. She has dark curls, she's slender, she's pretty, much older than Coco. She sees lines around her mouth. Laura likes to smile. She talks.

Coco carries on standing there and looks at the two people. They don't touch each other. They don't do anything strange, but she sees that Hans is happy. So that's what that looks like? When your boyfriend's happy. So that's what it looks like.

She sits down on the bench next to the tram stop and looks at the happy man. Hans leans forwards and looks at Laura. It seems like he is listening to her. He listens. He smiles. So that's what that looks like. When he listens. When he smiles. When he's happy.

All of a sudden she can't figure out whether she's seen this before or not. Has he ever looked at her in that way? Like that? She thinks about her mother with Martin, who embraced her and it looked natural. She thinks about her mother at the frame shop. She's been there a few times, not many. She has seen her mother's hands stroking wood. She was around seven. She couldn't keep her eyes off the fingers. The fingers slid very gently over the wood, looking for irregularities. She didn't pay attention to anyone around her. You could see that this was all she needed.

Laura gets up and goes to the counter. Hans watches her.

Coco gets up too and walks in the direction the tram came from. She knows that nobody is watching her.

So that's what it looks like. It rumbles on. Just like that other sentence. *Must have been in deep shock. Must have been in deep shock.*

Of course, that's what isn't right. It's been there in front of her nose for years, but she hasn't seen it. She has never seen her mother in panic. Her mother doesn't do panic. That's the lie. She wasn't panicking. She thought that her daughter was dying and she wasn't panicking. That's the whole story. That's all it is.

Does it matter? Am I someone else now? If my lover isn't happy with me, if my mother can do without me, am I someone else? *You are free. You are free. I'm relieving you. You are free.*

Coco walks through the city in the morning. Her footsteps are light. She is alone. She knows it. She doesn't find it disturbing.

It's a great relief to know that you are alone and that it's not a disturbing thought.

She looks at the black water in the canals. She is water and she mustn't stand still. Still water is unhealthy.

She fetches beer from the supermarket, six cans in plastic, and looks for a bench next to the canal.

She should be studying, yes, yet she doesn't really know why. She smiles because it's all right to think this—I don't know.

'Have you seen how many ribbons I have?' she says softly. That's all that will be left of her studies one day, a single sentence.

One can of beer leads the way to the next can of beer, like the way eating just makes her more hungry, sex makes her want more sex. Why even begin wanting anything?

'A lot of something. I don't like anything in particular but I do like a lot of something,' she says to a seagull above the canal. The beer makes her feel horny. The pubs are still closed. She wants to fuck.

'**WHAT ARE YOU** doing?' Martin asks.

'Maybe you should do it, I've so little strength left in my hands.'

'What are you doing?'

'The pain is pushing out from the inside, but if I press hard on my head, it gets less.'

'Shall I call someone?'

'Would you press?' She hears him get up. She doesn't open her eyes. She takes her hands away from her head. Then she feels his hands, two warm shells enclosing her skull.

'Press.' He presses.

'Harder.' He presses harder. Her body goes limp.

'Like that, yes.' Then he lets go. She opens her eyes. He has sat back down again.

'Should I call someone?'

'Who do you want to call then?'

'Is it getting worse—in your head?'

'OK now.'

'Should I call Coco?'

'Leave Coco for a bit.'

'How's she doing at uni?'

Elisabeth doesn't know the answer. She thinks. 'Her desk is here.'

'She was pretty tanked last time.'

'Yes,' she smiles, 'I didn't give her a hard time about it. You were there. You saw it.'

'Yes, I saw it.'

'Wasn't difficult, you know. I'm good at that. I can give people space. Wilbert too. I was very good at that, giving him space.'

'Your lips are dry, drink something.'

'I've never got in her way.' Martin doesn't say anything. Doesn't he believe her?

'You need to drink.'

'When she was three, she'd sleep really soundly, and sometimes I'd comb her hair then. And one time, I rubbed Nivea into her cheeks when she was sleeping.'

'You're not too scared to ask me to do things.' Martin smiles. 'I mean, why do you always dare to ask me for help?'

'You needed me. You couldn't do without me. I can work seven days a week if need be. I can do that.'

'You can do that.'

'You need me. The shop's nothing without me there.'

'Don't you think your daughter needs you?'

'If I work seven days a week, I can't very well look after a child, can I...? You were lucky with me.'

'You... you could have worked less.'

'You liked the fact I was always available.'

'... yes.'

'Yes, right?'

'Yes.' Martin looks pained.

'Only once when I tried to put socks on her in her sleep, then she woke up.'

'Why were you putting socks on her?'

'She kept kicking her covers off. I always have cold feet myself. I managed one foot, but the socks were too small. They grow fast. She began to kick and I thought: I'm almost there, it was almost on, I just need to grip that leg a little tighter.'

'And then?' Martin's eyes widen.

'You look worried.'

'And then?'

'Nothing, she woke up. Began to cry at once. Don't do

that, she cried. With such a contorted face. And so, *hup*, in one fell swoop that sleeping child was gone. *HUP.* Gone.'

'And what did you do then?'

'I got angry... But I didn't let it show at all. I know that she couldn't do anything about it, me being angry. I walked away quickly, because she couldn't do anything about it. I did understand. Now you have to press.'

'Aren't those pills for this?'

'I just have to lie down for a bit.'

'You're already lying down. I'm going to call someone now,' Martin says.

'Yes.'

THERE'S A HANDSOME man in the glass booth at the front of the casino. Next to him is a ficus tree.

'Do you want to fuck me?' Coco asks.

He frowns, says, 'I've got a break at twelve,' and then Coco's panic sets in. It's because of that very definite future moment in time. Then she knows that this lightness won't last. She doesn't even know whether the lightness will last twelve hours. She has to keep moving, things have to keep on happening.

'Twelve is too late,' she says, 'it has to be now, I don't know how things will be at twelve. That's quite a while ...' She tries to count the hours. He smiles.

'Sorry, pussycat, work comes before the ladies.'

'Work? You like your work?'

'What do you think, pussycat?'

'You find your work satisfying?'

'Huh?'

Coco looks around her, in search of other men. 'I want satisfying too,' she says. She spins on her heels. She sees boys, children practically.

She walks up and down past the slot machines. She has to keep on moving until she finds something to follow.

A man, an idea, a book, it doesn't matter what. But she can't go and lie down now there's nothing, now she doesn't have a new reason to get up again. Her phone rings, it's Martin. She goes outside.

'Your mother's not doing too well,' he says, 'perhaps you'd better come home.' She smiles. Her prayers were soon answered.

She goes back into the casino.

'Sorry,' she says to the man next to the ficus, 'I have to go, my mother is ill. She's dying. I have to hurry.'

Coco runs. She runs along the canals, she runs across the Overtoom, she runs past trams and taxis. She knows it's too far to run, but she runs. She has to get to her mother. How can Hans think that she doesn't want anything? How could she think that herself? She finds it so easy to want something. She wants to go to her mother and when she trips on the Rokin in front of the Maison de Bonneterie and her trousers stain red from the blood on her knees, she can only do a better job of showing how much she wants to run. The more wounded, the better; those who aren't afraid of falling run faster.

HALF OF HER vision is black. Elisabeth tilts her head, as though she'll be able to see the other half then, but one half remains black. She sees Coco. She turns her head. Only Coco.

Should I call someone, Martin had asked. She is sure she said 'Wilbert,' but now there's only Coco there.

Martin said, 'I'll leave the two of you alone.'

It's difficult to keep her eyes open, but she's afraid of closing them. She doesn't want to die while Coco is watching. She doesn't want to leave as a strange woman. No clients waiting in the salon. No witnesses. No drama.

She opens her eyes as wide as she can, the other half of the image is moving now. She tries to sit up.

'I'm feeling much better now,' she says, 'I just need to sleep a bit. Will you tell Martin that I'm going to have a short nap. OK?'

'Oh,' Coco says, as though she's disappointed.

How can she get the child to leave without offending her? She really does want Coco to be happy, naturally, she wants nothing else, but not here.

'I love you,' she says. It's a gift she's happy to give. Something she still had left over and didn't need any more herself.

'I love you too,' Coco replies smoothly. She sounds just like the hairdresser now. Then Coco laughs loudly. Elisabeth laughs too. Just going along with things is always the best.

'Sleep tight, fishwife.'

'Night-night, fish.'

Coco walks away. Voices in the hall. Front door. Coco's footsteps on the stairs.

A good ending to her own life, Elisabeth thinks, the same as she had once thought about her daughter's life, which had then just carried on. We need to leave it at this. Maybe she's right this time.

COCO IS SITTING on her bed and rocking her upper body back and forth. Keep moving.

For a very brief moment, Coco had thought: there she goes, these are my mother's last words: 'I love you.' It couldn't have been better. But when her mother said it, she hadn't looked at her. Her gaze was on the door, focussed not fleeting.

So Coco had nodded warmly to the dresser and said, 'I love you too.' Again it makes her laugh and think: if this wasn't so funny, you'd cry.

She mustn't lie down. This delirium can't bear sleep: all fat and heavy, hiding the lightness and pulling it down. She shouldn't have sent Martin away, now she's tied to this house and to waiting. Holding vigil is nothing for her. Something has to happen. Something with ambulances and doctors in the house and panic and pain, anything is better than this silence.

'I'm fed up with it,' she says and laughs at her own adolescent tone. When is she going to give up on this pretence of caring? No one asked for it. Someone has to do it. No one asked for it. Someone has to do it. She rocks along with the words. Someone has to do it, someone has to do it.

'You're incapable of saying no,' Hans had once said. Now she knows that she is capable of saying no, maybe she even wants to say no, but that something has to be asked of her before she can say no to it. No one wants anything from her, there's nothing she has to refuse, or can refuse. Maybe she should walk away, leave her mother to her fate. Forget the roster. Of course. She created it herself, what a wonderful creation. She has made herself indispensable here so that she can refuse now. She can go now and be missed. She exists. They'll have to look for her, they'll bring her back and then she'll cry out: I'm not doing it anymore. She realises at once though that they'll understand her, no one will try to contradict her, and she sits back down again.

Wait a minute, a moment will come when her mother asks her for something. Be alert now. It won't be much, pay attention.

ELISABETH LETS HER legs slip out of bed one last time. She hoists herself up on the rollator and stands. Her body wants to sink. She remains standing.

Elisabeth takes a step and tries not to think about how many more steps are needed. One step, she thinks, because that's all that needs to happen, and again, a single step. One single step. Only with the left foot. Only with the right foot. A single step. Time is nothing. Distance is nothing. Only with the left foot. Only with the right foot. A single step.

Oh, look, there's the threshold, there it is already. It's a friendly hairdresser's shop melody inside her head. Need any help? No, thank you. Can you manage? Oh, fine, you know. Whoops-a-daisy. There's the hall. Look at that. Whoops-a-daisy. One step.

It's like shaving wood. One sweep is nothing. Patience. She smells the sawdust, the shavings, she shaves and shaves and the natural wood comes to the surface by itself, the stairs appear by themselves.

Just a little sit down, wait a while, just a little.

Only breath. Only air. Some more air please, some more air please... Please!

Thank you. You're welcome. Anything else? One step up, there, up you go.

'What are you thinking about? What are you thinking about, Mum?'

Another step, I'm thinking: one more step.

'Darling, what are you thinking about? What's on your mind?'

One step is on my mind, one step, darling.

'But there must be more than...'

That's not how the song goes. That's not how it goes. Look. Stair rod. Copper. Just one more.

Landing.

Her cheek to the soft carpet, she inches herself slowly forwards like a worm. The head is too heavy to lift and she pushes it forwards and lets the body follow. There must be an easier way, to move forwards, but she doesn't know what it is.

COCO HEARS THE stairs creak and stops rocking. It's an old house. She rocks again, but again there's a noise. Unmistakeable. Now there a sound that's getting louder, something is coming closer.

'Mum?'

Of course not, her mother can't get up the stairs. It takes her twenty minutes just to get to the toilet. Coco rocks again and knows she has to leave this room, this house. There isn't enough space. Everything that can't really happen, because there isn't enough space for it, no oxygen, is happening now inside her head. She gets up, but before she's even taken a step she stops short.

It is real. It is slithering this way. Coco freezes and feels her heart beating. Something is happening. It's getting closer. She hears breathing now, it's not hers. Mum. No doubt about it.

Mum is coming to get her. She's coming to ask her. Now it's going to happen. Her mother needs her. Coco realises at once that all her thoughts just now were just boasting. She sinks slowly back down onto the bed, holds her breath, as though hers might chase away her mother's, her eyes peeled on the door. She doesn't blink.

I will be there, she says to herself. She senses that it's possible, she will be there for her mother.

Yes, she says.

You can't just decide to love someone.

Oh yes, I can. She decides.

COCO'S DOOR. GENTLY now, Liz. She rests her head against it. A mug's game. She could be discovered at any moment. Then the drama she's trying to avoid would ensue. Questions. Tears. Hugs, for Christ's sake.

Sit up now.

The key is still hanging on a hook on the doorframe. It's hanging there nicely. She's never hidden it. Never been difficult about it.

She nestles against the doorframe, raises herself up, takes the key from the hook, puts it in the lock, turns it, and sinks back down.

It feels like a hug. Her arms do what they can.

You're safe here, girl, be there, my little monster, be safe.

She hears love songs inside her head.

'How can something so wrong feel so right?'

SHE HEARD HER mother's body against her door. Coco hasn't dared to move. This time she won't be too much. Her mother will have to come herself, she will have to ask.

I won't move. I can be silent.

She'll do it well. Move with her, like a shadow. She won't feel anything, she promises that.

The slithering seems to be going away.

'Mama?' she whispers and then slaps herself in the face. Don't ask for anything.

Silence.

'Stupid bitch,' she says to herself, loudly and clearly. Your mother on the stairs. Your mother on a wooden raft. Christ, this room is too small for you. She gets up. It's almost twelve. The man next to the ficus is about to take his break. Very short black hair, he had. Shaved, but not because he was balding. Good hair. She goes over to the door. It's stuck. She pushes. The door doesn't open. She sinks to her knees, peers at the chink between the door and the post to see what's wrong with the lock.

Mum was here.

She stares at the lock for a long time, her mouth gaping. Her astonishment is great and leaves no room for thought. As the astonishment slowly wears off, she gets her phone out of her trouser pocket and looks at the thing, as though she can do as little about it as the locked door. Then she cries. Not because her mother has locked her up but because she so wants to tell someone her mother has done it and she doesn't know who. Of course she thinks of Hans, but Hans wants her to be angry with her mother and Coco doesn't feel any anger. She wants to tell it to someone who will become angry with her and who she can then look at and say, 'Calm down, it's not that bad.' Someone who cares about her, someone she can comfort.

ELISABETH LIES DOWN to die. She has to do it before midday. She breathes heavily towards it. Her breath gains a sound. A heavy, deep groaning sound she's never heard herself make before. It's the bass line of the hairdresser's shop melody. Aa-ooh. Aa-ooh. Aa-ooh. Whoops-a-daisy. How does it go. Off you go. Aa-ooh. Go his own way. You know it. Look at that. Aa-ooh. Up you go, up you go. Aa-ooh. Words like coins and the bass sawing through it.

She is still clinging onto life when the sun reaches the top of the houses on the other side of the street and pours in. She opens her eyes.

The wooden table in the middle of the room is surrounded by light. She wants to touch the warm wood, she can already feel it in her right hand, though it doesn't move. Wanting to stroke the table top is enough. She doesn't do anything. She can't do anything. Only her eyes follow the light as it designates objects and embraces them. There's an old Duralex glass on the stool next to her bed. The sun lights up every minute scratch, exposing years and years with a single touch. She sees this as her blood slowly comes to a standstill.

Without moving her lips, she says, Now I no longer have a heart. She breathes air out one more time. She has managed it. She has gone alone.

COCO CALLS THE landline, sitting with her back to the closed door. The telephone rings, once, twice, three times, four times, only at the fifth ring does Coco realise that she has failed again, she has managed once again not to ask her mother anything. She gets up and stomps her way back to her bed.

THE PHONE IN the sitting room rings. The body on the bed in front of the window doesn't react. Elisabeth sees it.

From up on the left. Death is in the top left-hand corner of every room. She has stared there often, but never seen anything. Now the corner has swallowed her up and offers her new perspectives.

The world is changing fast. The sitting room fills up with every object from her life that has ever been broken or lost. The plastic inflatable Barbapapa set she gave Coco for her third birthday is on the wooden table, which doesn't have any scratches anymore. All nine of them fully inflated. It is as though the toys she once gave Coco are back in her possession. She smells the new plastic. The little rubber boat is lying next to the bed. The inflatable seal is upright at the foot of the bed. The floor fills up with all the beach balls she ever owned as child and mother, and now they won't be carried off by the wind. The room expands as only happens in dreams, making space for everything. So now it's complete.

The only thing missing is a longing to tell someone about the beauty of all these objects.

Only the body on the bed is not lovely and new. It contrasts sharply with the shiny, blue, blow-up animal at the foot of the bed. Elisabeth observes it with discomfort, as though it's one of her daughter's toys she has accidentally dropped and broken. The daughter's warm big body she once brought into life is not far from the broken corpse.

Elisabeth can see into Coco's room too, she can see everything.

Coco sits on her bed, telephoning.

She says, 'It's me. I don't want to bother you, but Mum has locked me up. I can't get out.'

'Yes, she still can. Apparently.'

'I can't reach anyone, you only have to open the door for me. I'll throw down the keys. Sorry.'

'Maybe it's the morphine, it can make people go weird.'

Then Coco lets herself fall back on the bed, the telephone still in her hand.

When she was two, she would sleep holding a book. When she was four, it was an old flannel. When she was six, she sat on the back of the bike clutching a naked Barbie to her chest.

Elisabeth sees everything that ever existed. From Coco's first wooden cot to the black metal teenager's bed on which she semi-reclines so awkwardly now, tapping her phone rhythmically against the headboard. She sees the flowery fitted sheet on which Coco was born, but also the stiff white cotton of the hospital bed where she herself arrived in the world —to her deathbed, which is still warm.

Her new world is filled only with things, but that doesn't mean she doesn't know about everything that happened to those things: who owned them, who carried them, who loved them, and who broke them. Nothing escapes her or has ever escaped her, as her daughter and her father prove, with their hands and their mouths and their jitteriness.

The girl just keeps on tapping her phone and doesn't notice the scratches appearing on the metal headboard.

It doesn't matter anymore: in Elisabeth's world everything she broke and spoiled will rise up again, spotless. Everything is whole and pretty and new in the showroom of her life, every mattress un-slept on.

She sees everything. She sees the tram rails, wet from the rain on the day she visited her daughter in hospital. They cut diagonal stripes across her body and coloured them in with rust. When she talked about that day to Wilbert later, she had to stop herself from mentioning the rails.

They wanted to call her a number of sickly names, but she refused them. Ugly names she never wants to say out loud, but the tram rails remain.

She can arrange the things by function or size. First she is tempted to group them by material: wood with wood, plastic with plastic. She suspects there are infinite ways of ordering them, but, before she gets lost in the game, her daughter taps her back into time. Her little Nokia is getting damaged by the tapping too. Coco doesn't notice.

Her daughter sits up. She gets up and stamps across the floor. She knows that the chandelier is hanging right underneath her. She stamps harder. The chandelier shakes, the glass droplets sway gently, projecting tiny sparkles onto the dead body.

I'LL STAMP UNTIL I fall through, everything is possible. Coco thinks she hears the bell, but doesn't feel like being quiet now. Hans can't have got here that fast. She jumps up and down with both feet, she knows she's exactly above the old chandelier. The bell again. Yes, the bell. So Mum isn't opening the door, she's feigning ignorance.

Coco goes over to the window, opens it, leans out and sees the hairdresser. She's never seen the hairdresser outside of the hair salon. Too intimate, she thinks, the hairdresser on the loose like that. The hairdresser rings the bell again.

'Hello,' she calls.

'Hi, Coco, we had an appointment at half past eleven, didn't we?'

'Was that today?'

'Yes.'

'Oh. I think she's asleep.'

'Doesn't she know I'm coming?'

'A surprise.'

'I've only got half an hour.'

'Oh, right, I'm coming—oh—wait—she's locked me in.'

'Who?'

'Elisabeth.'

'Locked you in?'

'Yes.'

'You're kidding?'

'She really has.'

'Blimey.'

'I think she's hallucinating, because of her head and that.'

'Has it already got to her head?'

'What did you say?'

'I said,' the hairdresser is almost shouting now, 'has—it—got—to—her—head—already?'

'Yeah, sure.'

'Christ, Coco.'

'Ye-ah.'

'I don't have much time.'

'Oh yeah, sorry, I'll throw down the front door key.'

'LIZ?' THE HAIRDRESSER is the only person who abbreviates her name. He opens the door cautiously. When he sees her lying on the bed in front of the window, he sees at once that everything that could happen to this body has already happened.

'Jesus,' the hairdresser says. 'Oh, Liz.'

She spotted him a while ago, in front of the door in his leather jacket. She'd never seen her hairdresser wearing a coat before. He doesn't come closer. He turns around and leaves the room. He'll fetch Coco.

Now she's alone for an instant. No, that's not right. She's everywhere. The body on the bed is alone.

Something's wrong.

NO.

It comes from the belly to the breast, the wave. NO. She doesn't have a body anymore, why still the sensations in it? The things, she has to go back to the things, but she's trapped in a wave. They, the others, would call it fear, they'd call it anger, Elisabeth is sure of it. They would give it the names of unidentifiable matters and forget that it's a wave that is filling her body and pounding against the walls. Call it fear, she'd wish she wasn't afraid; call it anger, she'd wish she wasn't angry. She calls it a wave and wishes the sea didn't exist, not in her, but the water pounds and wants to get out. The hairdresser is already walking up the stairs as her body sighs one last time.

'COCO?' THE HAIRDRESSER calls out on the landing.

'Here! The room at the front.' The hairdresser turns the key, which is still in the lock, and opens the door to her bedroom.

The hairdresser wearing a jacket. He is carrying a small leather bag.

'Thank you.'

'Yes.'

'How is she?'

The hairdresser gulps and says, 'I'm afraid I was too late.'

'Too late?'

'Dead... I'm afraid.'

Coco realises straight away that the hairdresser is right. 'Fucking hell,' she takes an enormous step towards the hairdresser, who is blocking the doorway. The hairdresser jumps and hops to the left, but Coco wants to go that way too.

'Oh,' the hairdresser says as he steps to the right. Coco runs across the landing and rushes down the stairs as fast as she can, as though she wants to catch up with her mother. The hairdresser follows her. The doorbell rings.

'Mum!' Coco shouts in the hall.

AS THE SOUNDS of the hairdresser's footsteps on the stairs slowly fade away, Elisabeth vanishes into the things.

The veneer on the dresser is immaculate. The linen cupboard no longer has an old Donald Duck sticker on it. The side table no longer wobbles. This is it.

There's a green wine glass on the side table. Elisabeth waits for the memory. Her memory is flawless. It's a goblet from a bygone age. A fat foot under a small, round glass.

No.

She would have known this.

She looks around and sees: glass fruit bowl, no longer a chip out of it, yes, hers. Bredemeijer teapot, immaculate shine, yes, her teapot. Suede slippers, absolutely hers, this is her heaven. Green goblet, no. No, not hers.

Is there always something wrong, even in heaven? Perhaps she isn't dead yet? Perhaps she has to share it, the heaven. No, that can't be true. That telephone on the bedside cabinet, that's not hers. Coco?

She's not dead yet. That must be it. First her death has to be established, that'll be it.

'Nothing happens without paperwork,' she hears Martin cry out. She has to call Martin, he arranges everything.

Coco isn't fast with those things, of course. The news still has to be passed on. What a business. Coco, hurry up. The eyes are still open, of course, the mouth too. Get packing, tidy it away. Come on now.

And then, when she thought she didn't have a body

anymore, when she hoped to be so much further on than she is, Elisabeth feels her own hands very lightly on her stomach. She hasn't lost her body yet.

Her daughter is moving in her, she's never left her belly. The movements soon become fainter. A little while, and then Elisabeth won't have a body anymore, no belly left, no child, and now she knows that she's afraid.

IN HER FINAL steps towards her mother, she just manages to think: yes, it's quite clear, even though it's the first dead person she's seen. She shakes her head indignantly and automatically takes the arm that is hanging out of the bed and lays it on her mother's stomach, the other hand on top. The body is clammy and heavy. She can't remember the last time she touched this body, but it's never been easier than now.

She closes her mother's eyes and speaks in the voice of a doll's mother: 'Oh, dear Mummy,' again she shakes her head. She pushes her mother's chin down. The mouth falls open again. She takes the sheet and pulls it up to under her mother's chin, forcing the mouth shut with it. She tucks in the sides tightly.

'There, that's better.' She hears the contented tone in her voice, as though she's been waiting for this, this manageable mother.

'Shall I leave you alone?' Coco looks around. The hairdresser is standing behind her, next to him is Hans.

'I let him in.'

'Yes, the hairdresser was there already,' she says, 'I'd forgotten, sorry.'

'Or can I do anything for you?' the hairdresser asks.

'You'll stay for a cup of coffee though, won't you?' Coco asks him.

'I've got half an hour.'

Her mother's mouth stays nicely shut. Her hands are dry. Coco gently rubs a finger over a hand.

'Have you got her doctor's number?' Hans asks.

'Shall I call the doctor?' the hairdresser asks. 'I know her doctor.'

'Do we have to?'

'The doctor has to certify it,' Hans says.

'Well, this is something a hairdresser can certify too. I'll make coffee.' Coco goes to the kitchen. Hans follows her.

He says, 'Just call,' to the hairdresser.

'Do we have to right away? Get the doctor?' Coco asks in the kitchen.

'Have you called your father already?'

'What do you mean?'

'Your mother is dead.'

'Yes, that's quite obvious.'

'Sit down for a moment.'

'Thank you for coming, but the hairdresser had got here already, I'd forgotten about that.'

'So you said, yes.'

'Yes.'

'Are you drunk?'

'Laura seems really nice, by the way.'

'Sorry?'

'I saw you, in the Coffee Company.'

'Oh.'

'Christ.'

'What?'

'I'm starting to feel very light-headed.'

'You all right?'

'Fine, thank you.'

'I'll make the coffee,' Hans says.

'Top left cupboard, tin with the blue windmills, coffee filters are next to it.'

Hans fills the kettle.

'Six level scoopfuls for a whole pot. Or aren't you having coffee?'

Hans gets a filter, two of them, one falls on the floor. He doesn't notice.

'You've dropped one.'

He looks at the floor, bends down, and picks it up. 'I think you'd better go and sit down now.'

'It's fine, Hans.'

'That's what you think.'

Coco laughs, 'Next you'll be saying I must have been in deep shock.'

The hairdresser enters the kitchen. 'The doctor's on his way.'

'Thank you,' Hans says.

'I'll leave you alone.'

'I'll call you,' Coco says, 'I need to make an appointment.'

'Haven't decided to grow it back then?'

'What do you think?'

'You shouldn't have it so short... could trim the ends, though.'

'Yes, I'll call you... perhaps a different colour?'

The hairdresser holds out his hand. She takes it in both of hers.

'Condolences.'

'Yes,' Coco says, 'condolences. You too. Mum always liked going to the salon.'

The hairdresser shakes Hans's hand. 'Condolences to you too.'

'Thank you.'

The hairdresser leaves. 'I'll see myself out.'

She watches him go. 'That poor hairdresser,' Coco says.

'Poor hairdresser?'

'Finding that dead woman.'

'Your mother, you mean.'

'Who else?'

'You feel sorry for the hairdresser.'

'You go out in the morning to give someone a quick cut... and get this.'

'You don't have to think about the hairdresser.'

'But I *am* thinking about the hairdresser! Fucking hell, I am thinking about the hairdresser!' Coco is crying.

'Oh, sweetheart.' He puts his arms around her.

She pushes him away. 'I'm crying because I'm not allowed to think about the hairdresser, Hans. Because you won't let me think about the hairdresser, because I can never do things right.'

'Sorry.' The coffee percolates. 'What are thinking about now?'

She hesitates. 'The hairdresser didn't have any coffee.'

Elisabeth is dead.

THE DOCTOR SPEAKS in a hushed voice. 'Time of death.' He pushes up his sleeve and looks at his watch: 'Eleven fifty-five.' Hans and her father look at their watches now too. Coco doesn't have a watch and looks at the kitchen clock. The doctor writes.

'Her Christian names?'

'Elisabeth Johanna,' her father says. He is sitting next to the doctor at the kitchen table. Hans pours the coffee.

While Hans was letting her father in, Coco had filled a large coffee mug with port. She clutches the mug in both hands as though letting the coffee warm them and drinks it calmly.

The doctor had just been through to her mother when her father arrived. He had cast a hasty glance around the room and followed the doctor immediately into the kitchen.

Hans leans on the counter and looks at his feet.

He's bored, Coco thinks, he's waiting. You don't walk away right after fucking someone, you wait a couple of days—so what about a dead mother?

'Oh Hans,' she says. He looks up. He doesn't look happy. She'll have to help him to leave her. He isn't good at it.

'Can I do anything for you?' Hans asks, 'Sort out anything?'

'Martin is arranging everything.'

'Has anyone called him yet?'

'No.'

'Should I call him?'

'If you're happy to, you should do it.'

She puts the empty coffee mug down on the counter

and opens the smallest kitchen drawer. Between the sandwich bags, elastic bands, kitchen and aluminium foil, there's a pot of Nivea. It's been there for as long as she can remember.

She takes her mother's hand as though for a manicure. The hand is damp and heavy. Taking extra care, she spreads the cream, rubs it into the fingers, kneads gently. She hums.

When she has finished the second hand, she notices how greasy the hands now look and wonders whether you can put cream on a dead body. Can the skin absorb the cream? Or—she smiles at the thought—this would be typical of her mother, is she made of something different from other mothers? She can't get the smile off her face.

The sun is at its meridian and no longer enters through the sunroom windows. I can go through there, Coco thinks, I've already proved it. She rubs the scar on her neck. Glass in the carotid artery. Rubbish, it's not that quick. Anyone can go through a window. But who does it deliberately? Happily? On purpose? She wasn't clumsy, not as a child and not now, either; she knew what she was doing. It was autumn.

Coco knows full well that the lightness will cease. This smile cannot keep spreading, the sun cannot climb any higher.

She walks to the threshold, as far from the sunroom window as possible, it's her house now. Maybe she can call Herman Siezen. Hassle, even the thought is exhausting. There you have it again. Don't get tired. She can do anything now. Now. She has to hurry up. She is realistic, being able to do anything is always a temporary state.

With thanks to Danielle Vidal, Eduard van Hulsen, and everyone at L'Encadreur BV.

On the Design

As book design is an integral part of the reading experience, we would like to acknowledge the work of those who shaped the form in which the story is housed.

Tessa van der Waals (Netherlands) is responsible for the cover design, cover typography and art direction of all World Editions books. She works in the internationally renowned tradition of Dutch Design. Her bright and powerful visual aesthetic maintains a harmony between image and typography and captures the unique atmosphere of each book. She works closely with internationally celebrated photographers, artists, and letter designers. Her work has frequently been awarded prizes for Best Dutch Book Design.

The 'Kissing Fish' picture on the cover was taken by photographer Claro Cortes IV (Philippines) on Valentine's Day 2005 at a small pet shop in Shanghai. Locally, the aquarium fish is known as 'jie wen yu' and actually puckers its lips when facing another fish; it is a popular gift during Valentine's Day in China. The photo was among Reuters Top Pictures of the Day. For the cover it has been rotated by 90 degrees.

The cover has been edited by lithographer Bert van der Horst of BFC Graphics (Netherlands).

Suzan Beijer (Netherlands) is responsible for the typography and careful interior book design of all World Editions titles.

The text on the inside covers and the press quotes are set in Circular, designed by Laurenz Brunner (Switzerland) and published by Swiss type foundry Lineto.

All World Editions books are set in the typeface Dolly, specifically designed for book typography. Dolly creates a warm page image perfect for an enjoyable reading experience. This typeface is designed by Underware, a European collective formed by Bas Jacobs (Netherlands), Akiem Helmling (Germany), and Sami Kortemäki (Finland). Underware are also the creators of the World Editions logo, which meets the design requirement that 'a strong shape can always be drawn with a toe in the sand.'